THE STARFISH TALISMAN

LARK GRIFFING

WIND LARK
PUBLISHING

ISBN-10: 10: 0-9988719-2-3

ISBN-13: **978-0-9988719-2-9**

Edited by Wing Family Editing

*This book is for my mother,
who saw the wolves under the
dining room table.*

CHAPTER 1

*R*eagan sat in the back seat of her mother's car staring out the window. She hadn't spoken more than two sentences to her mom in two days, and she wasn't going to sit up front riding shotgun with her, either. If her mom was going to be a traitor, dumping her only daughter at an aunt's house for the summer, an aunt she didn't even know, then this daughter wasn't going to make it any easier on the mom in question. This whole situation was unfair and completely unacceptable. How could her mother expect her to be happy about this? Nope, Mom was going to suffer.

"Reagan, how long are you going to keep this up?" asked her mother, Becky. "I can't help this situation. I need to travel for work. You can't come, and you can't stay by yourself, so this is the best solution. I'm just grateful that your aunt is willing to take you in. I haven't spoken to your father's sister in years."

"Exactly," Reagan burst out loudly, forgetting her vow of silence. "I don't know this woman. You don't know this woman, but you are dumping me there without a clue. The woman could be a serial killer."

"Don't be silly. Women aren't serial killers. Honey, it's not like

1

she's a stranger. We fell out of touch, but your father loved her dearly."

"Okay, Daddy loved her. Daddy loved everybody and everything. Hell, he probably would have loved his sister even if she was a serial killer."

"You're right, he would have, and don't say 'hell'," scolded her mom.

Reagan resisted the urge to scream "hell, hell, hell" at the top of her lungs. She was miserable, but this really wasn't making her feel any better. Sighing, she slithered over the back of the front seat so that she could land next to her mother on the passenger side, a move she had perfected on those rides home from school with her friends.

"What the hell are you doing?" her mother squealed protecting the steering wheel from Reagan's left foot. "Are you trying to get us killed?"

"At least we'd be together, and don't say 'hell'," quipped her still pouting daughter.

"Don't be morbid, dear," said Becky as she turned and gave her daughter a half smile. At least her daughter was talking to her. She would take it even if it was macabre.

"I don't even know this aunt, and who the hell, heck names their kid Willow?" asked Reagan, shaking her head in wonderment.

"The same people who named your father Wolf. Seriously, you knew your grandparents were the original hippies. We've told you that."

"I know you said that, but I never met my grandparents, and I don't know this Willow-chick, either. Does she do drugs?"

"No, for heaven's sake, she does not do drugs," said Becky, but she did look worried for a second. "She's an adult and an artist who supports herself and doesn't do drugs or anything."

Reagan looked at her mom, reading the worry lines on her forehead.

"Well, she probably only smokes weed, so that'd be okay," said Reagan, waiting a beat for the light slap upside the head that she figured would come from her mom. Becky tousled Reagan's hair and sighed.

"I am really sorry, honey. I know you don't want to do this. Neither do I, but I don't have a choice. We need to live. They said I'd be gone for three months, tops. I told them that wasn't good enough, that I'd need to be home in time to take you home for school, and they agreed. I'm sorry. It's my job, and the way we survive, so I have to do what I've got to do. You understand, don't you?"

Reagan nodded her head. She really did understand. It was just the two of them, and her mom worked hard to make ends meet. They weren't poor, but they weren't rolling in the dough. Her mom had made a lot of sacrifices for Reagan, so it was Reagan's turn to suck it up.

"I understand, and I will try to stay positive. I'm not happy about it, and I'm not going to lie. This is the summer before my senior year. I will miss all that time with my friends."

"I know, but on the other hand, Kaylee is going to be living and working at Cedar Point all summer, and didn't you tell me that Bonnie is going to spend the summer with her father in Florida? That leaves Gail. Didn't she just get a job?"

Reagan nodded, sighing. Her mom didn't even need to ask the question. Reagan had been moaning about those very things only two weeks before. Still, she would have been able to see them some of the time. She could have gone to Cedar Point, and Gail wasn't going to work 24/7. Now, she was going to be stuck in some stupid small town on the coast of Maine, in some stupid house, with her stupid aunt, with the stupid name of Willow. It was all just … stupid.

CHAPTER 2

I think this is the right address," Becky said, peering at the faded numbers on the mailbox post. The box was at the end of a long, curving gravel drive that disappeared into a hall of trees, their boughs meeting each other over the lane shrouding it in a dappled green dusk.

"Up that? I don't see a house or anything. This dirt road just disappears into the woods. In fact, I haven't seen any houses, or McDonald's or Starbucks, or Taco Bell, or a freaking mall. Mom? What the hell, shoot, heck?"

"You are going to owe me money. Do I have to start the swear jar again?"

"Sure. If you remember correctly, the last time you ended up paying me," retorted Reagan good-naturedly. She wasn't happy about her current situation, though. What was she going to do all summer? "Mom, do you think there's WiFi, or a library, or something?" Reagan asked nervously.

"I'm sure there is. It's not like you're on another planet. It'll be fine. I'm sure it will." Reagan glanced at her mom fully aware that it sounded like her mom was not only trying to convince her, but she was working on convincing herself.

Becky turned the car up the lane, driving under the bower of trees. The car bumped along the pockmarked road, dust rising behind it in clouds. The road curved several times before it exited the trees. Both Becky and her daughter gasped in surprise. The lane ran along the edge of a cliff, the ocean spread out to the east below the drop off. At the end of the lane, on the edge of the cliff, perched an enormous house, sadly in need of paint, with a wide front porch and an abundance of mullioned windows. Riotous colors splashed the flower beds in front of the porch, unconventional, with no rhyme or reason to the design.

"Wow," said Reagan, "I'm glad you told me Aunt Willow is a potter and not a painter."

"Why's that?" Becky asked, still staring at the house in awe.

"Because the paint job on that house sucks!" exclaimed Reagan. Becky sighed as she continued up the driveway, passing the house on her left and pulling into a gravel pad in front of a large faded barn. She parked next to an old minivan with a Tide Pool Pottery logo on the driver's side door.

"Well, I guess this is it. We're here. It looks like your aunt has plenty of room for you. It's not like you'll be cramped," Reagan's mom announced with forced cheerfulness. Reagan just rolled her eyes and opened the car door to step out. An explosion of barking caused her to snatch her foot back in to the car, slamming the door. She peered out the window to see a yellow Lab streaking toward the car, ears flapping, mouth open, teeth glinting, baying loudly at them. Reagan and her mom looked at each other.

"I'm not moving," said Reagan, eyeing the big dog planted outside her door.

"I second that," said Becky, trying to figure out what to do next without looking terrified and not in control. A figure emerged from the barn.

"Wiley, out." Immediately, the dog sat, panting a happy smile. The figure gestured for Reagan and her mom to open the door. Reagan shook her head 'no'. Sighing, the figure moved toward the car, whistling for the dog to come. Wiley trotted to his master's side and sat, looking like a happy clown and not the killer he resembled moments ago.

"Come on, let's do this," said Becky. Reagan hesitated, then opened the door and stepped out. "Willow? It's been a very long time." Becky moved toward the woman with the dog. Reagan held back, watching the exchange.

"Hello, Becky." The woman's raspy voice was strong and commanding. "Come here, girl. I could pick you out as Wolf's daughter anywhere. Well, come on, Wiley won't hurt you. Go say hello, Wiley." The dog obediently walked to Reagan, sat, and offered a paw. Reagan laughed despite her remaining fear. "Well, pet him. Let him know you like him." Reagan hesitantly stretched out a hand. The dog tensed. Becky tensed. Reagan almost dropped her hand, but instead reached for the dog's soft ears. She rubbed gently behind his right ear. Wiley moaned and leaned hard into her hand, insisting on a hardy rub.

"Well, that worked out all right. Wiley thinks you're okay. Why don't you take your things into the house? I have to finish something in the barn. If I stop now, it'll be ruined. I'll join you in just a few minutes." Reagan and Becky looked at each other a little uncomfortably. They both felt weird just going into a stranger's house. "Don't be silly, Reagan, you're going to live here all summer, so you might as well make yourself at home. Just go on in. Pick yourself a bedroom upstairs on the third floor. Any bedroom will be fine. There are sheets for the beds in the dressers in each room. Take your pick. Just stay off the fourth floor. You have no need to go up there. Besides, it isn't safe. Becky, are you staying the night? If so, grab yourself a bedroom and make yourself at home. I'll be in a bit." With that, Willow spun on her heels and disappeared back in the barn. Wiley watched her leave but decided to stick with Reagan.

"Okay, that was creepy," said Reagan.

"Don't overreact. Your aunt has been living alone for a lot of years. Her social skills are a bit rusty that's all. Let's grab your stuff out of the trunk." They each grabbed two suitcases, and Reagan shouldered her backpack as they started toward the house, Wiley trotting happily behind them.

"Mom, what did Aunt Willow mean when she said the fourth floor is dangerous?" asked Reagan as she peered at the house, looking intently at the row of windows on the fourth floor.

"My guess is that some of the house might be in disrepair. She just doesn't want you getting hurt in an area of the house she doesn't use. That's all I can figure." Reagan nodded, thinking it made sense. She glanced up again at the old house and was surprised to see a face peering out of the middle fourth floor window. She squinted against the sun and looked more closely. No, there was nothing there. She laughed at herself. Her imagination was running wild.

CHAPTER 3

*R*eagan and her mom mounted the steps to the wide front porch. A swing hung at the far end, and there were four white rocking chairs lined up the length of the porch. Becky sighed at the sight of them.

"I could sit down in one of those chairs and stay a lifetime," she said.

"Why don't you, Mom?" teased Reagan.

"You know I don't want to leave you, but I don't know what else to do," said Becky, exasperated.

"I know. I'm sorry. I was just teasing, but I do see myself planted in a rocking chair a lot this summer or curled up on that porch swing with a good book or ten." All of a sudden, the summer didn't look so bad. What could be wrong with spending the summer reading on a porch of an old creepy house on the ocean cliffs in Maine? Determined to have a better attitude, Reagan opened the old screen door and stepped into the past.

They entered a central hall which was on the second floor of the house, the half-subterranean first floor a flight below. An open stairwell wound up and up, past the third floor to the fourth which disappeared in a dusty darkness. On the left, just past the first step, was what looked like a parlor or sitting room. To the right of the open hall was a room that looked like it might be an office. Straight ahead, the hall opened into a grand dining room with a table that seated fourteen guests. Large built in buffets and china cabinets flanked the walls. Straight through to the back, they caught a glimpse of a giant kitchen, the doors propped open to allow access. Wiley shot past them, his nails clicking on the gleaming hardwood. He entered the tiled kitchen floor where they could hear his noisy lapping as he watered his thirst.

They were still taking in his surroundings as Wiley made his way back to them, his jowls running with water, dripping on the polished floor. Becky's mom whistled a low tone.

"Wow, this place is amazing. Your dad always said that the homestead was a blast from the past, but this is incredible. The antiques in here must be worth a fortune."

"The outside of the house really doesn't tell the tale of the inside, does it, Mom? I feel like I'm going to be living in a museum or something. Is there any place to kick back and put your feet up? Everything is so formal. I mean, I just met Aunt Willow, but she doesn't look like the type to live in a place like this."

"Maybe there is another room that is more relaxing," said Becky. "Let's go settle you into a bedroom."

They picked up the bags and started up the stairs. Wiley bounded ahead of them, leading the way. When they reached the third floor, they could turn to the left, the right, or drop down a step and go straight down a narrow hall. This was the only hall with a door that could close.

"That part of the house looks different from this part. I think that might have been the servants' quarters."

"That's crazy," said Reagan. "Can we check it out?"

"I don't see why not."

They left the suitcases in the main hall and stepped down the single step into the narrow passage in front of them. On either side of the hall were small bedrooms. Many of them were barren, but several had small beds and a wash stand. At the very end of the hall was a narrow steep staircase that led downstairs.

On the right, before the staircase, was a bedroom fitted with a simple bed, a modern dresser, and a TV mounted on the wall. The bedspread was an Indian batik print, and the windows had shutters instead of curtains that could open or shut tight. There were a set of shelves that held several pieces of exquisite pottery.

"I think this might be your Aunt Willow's room. I feel like we're intruding. Come on."

They made their way back down the narrow hall to the wide open main hall in the front of the house. It was so much cheerier here, with white wainscoting and gleaming, polished bannisters. They grabbed the luggage and started looking through the rooms, feeling a bit like interlopers.

The first door they opened revealed a room that had two windows and faced the south side of the house. It had a twin bed and was decorated in light greens and yellows. Wiley walked in and stuck his wet nose to the window, looking out over his property. It was a cheery room, but Reagan moved on.

The second room was painted navy blue with white woodwork. A dark maple bedroom set furnished the space. A model of a racing sailboat graced a high shelf over the bed. Becky wondered aloud if it was Wolf's old room. As she looked around the room that may have once belonged to her husband, Wiley came in and flopped down on the braided rug in the middle of the floor. His tail thumped happily as Reagan gave his ears a couple of good scratches while she waited patiently for her mom to examine the other knick-knacks on the shelf.

The third room had rose and white wallpaper and a white chenille bedspread which covered an old-fashioned white iron bed. Despite the beautiful appointments, the room had a gloomy chill to it. Wiley stood out in the hall and whined, refusing to come in.

"What's the matter Wiley, too feminine for your tastes?" teased

Reagan. Wiley looked at her and gave his tail a tentative wag, then turned and led the way down the hall. He nosed his way into a room at the front of the house. When Reagan laid her eyes on the room, she knew it was the one she was going to pick.

The creamy white woodwork gleamed in a sharp contrast to the cornflower blue walls. A white four poster bed complete with a canopy was the main focal point. A small set of gleaming steps sat next to the bed to assist the occupant because the mattress was unusually high. A dresser and a highboy were along one wall, and a delicate writing desk was pushed up to a window so the writer could look out and gaze upon the ocean. The polished wooden floor was partially covered with a needlepoint woolen rug, predominately cornflower blue with touches of yellow and cream. An upholstered rocking chair sat in the corner, also canted so that the rocker had a majestic view of the ocean. Wiley sniffed around the room and then sat in front of Reagan, offering his paw as if to say that this was the right choice for her. Indeed, it was.

"This is it," said Reagan, delighted at the beauty and the view of the room. "I wonder why Aunt Willow doesn't use this beautiful room. It must have the best view in the entire house."

"It's a lovely room. It's the one I would choose if I was going to spend a summer here. Wiley seems to like it." Now, Wiley was stretched out on his side in a patch of sunshine, his tail thumping slowly at the mention of his name.

Reagan brought her suitcases into the room and began unpacking. At first, she was hesitant to put her clothes in the dressers, thinking the room hadn't been used in some time, but she discovered the place was spotless. Not a speck of dust had settled anywhere. Finding a set of blue and yellow flowered sheets, Reagan quickly made up the bed with the help of her mom.

"Where are you going to stay tonight? You are staying tonight, right?"

"Yes, I'm going to stay the night, but we need to leave early in the morning to get me to the airport on time. You still want to drive me so you can have the car, right?"

"Yeah, I'll die if I don't have a way to go places. Thanks, Mom. Now let's get you settled for the night. Which room do you want?"

"Your dad's, the navy-blue room. I just know that your father spent time in there. I can feel it."

Reagan helped her mom make up her bed, and then they both went down the stairs, not too sure what to do next. When they reached the bottom of the stairs, Wiley ran ahead to the kitchen, wiggling his butt happily. They followed him to discover that Aunt Willow was sitting at the table in the big country kitchen drinking a can of Pepsi. She gestured to the refrigerator and said, "Help yourself." Reagan gratefully raided the fridge, grabbing a Pepsi for herself. Her mother shook her head no and asked Willow where she could find a glass to have some water.

"We only have tap water. It's cold spring water from the deep well. You will find it is sweet and refreshing. The glasses are in the cupboard, right of the sink." She didn't make a move to play hostess and help. Reagan liked that about her. It made her feel more at home. Willow interrupted that thought, uncannily referring to it. "You'll find that I am not the greatest hostess. I figure you're a big girl who wears big girl pants. You can take care of yourself and find your way. I won't wait on you, nor do I expect you to wait on me. I have to warn you, I keep strange hours. When I feel creative, I may work all day and all night. You may not see me. You'll be left to your own devices. If you're both okay with that, this will work out. If not, we may all be miserable."

Becky looked startled, her mouth dropping open, but Reagan laughed. She was thinking that this actually might be okay.

"I am perfectly capable of taking care of myself. I can cook and do my own laundry. Mom is leaving me the car, so I can go when I need to. I will be happy to help you with whatever you need, but I certainly have no trouble leaving you alone."

Becky stared at the two of them. Willow and Reagan were looking at each other rather defiantly, yet with admiration.

"Great," said Becky, "you are both stubborn and independent. This will either work out well, or I will come back and find that you've killed each other!"

"It's not me you have to worry about," Willow said cryptically. Becky thought Willow was referring to Reagan, but Reagan felt a stir of fear in her gut. Willow held Reagan's eyes with her gaze, "Remember, stay off of the fourth floor." Reagan's gut tightened, butterflies started to flutter.

"Reagan isn't the type to break rules. Don't worry. She understands that you have some areas that are off limits, that might have fallen into disrepair, although I have to say, this house is beautifully kept. Did you restore it yourself?" asked Becky.

"There was nothing to restore. The house has been the same since my great-great-great-grandparents built it, other than the fact that the exterior needs a new coat of paint. The coastal weather is hard on the place, but the house is resilient. Okay, I need to go back to my studio. I figured we would order some pizza for dinner if that is okay with you. If you want, you can run into town and pick it up. That way Reagan can get a lay of the land, and I can get some work done. When you get hungry, head down the road and turn right on Starling Road. Take that straight into town. Antonio's Pizza is on the corner of the square. The library is on the square, too. I expect you will want to get some books to read. It'll be a long summer."

With that, Willow tossed the empty can into the recycling bin and headed out the kitchen door, leaving Reagan and her mom staring at each other, flabbergasted.

CHAPTER 4

*a*fter the kitchen encounter with Aunt Willow, Reagan retreated upstairs to grab her purse so she and her mom could drive to town. While in her bedroom, she decided she wanted the ocean breeze to invade her room. She slid the old, heavy windows open allowing the wind to blow the curtains inward. Peering out the window, she could see a path that led to the edge of the cliff. It looked as if it descended to the rocks and the ocean below. After she dropped off her mom in the morning, she was going to explore that path.

Reagan turned and started to walk out of the room. The corner of her eye caught a movement, and she turned, startled, but she only saw her own reflection in the old mirror. The curtains stirred in the breeze. That must be what I saw, thought Reagan as she headed out the door.

Reagan followed Willow's directions to town, driving down Starling Road while her mother rested in the passenger seat. Reagan rolled down the window letting the salty sea air blow her long brown hair and breathed deeply. She liked the tangy ocean scent. It felt so much different here than the sticky, humid Ohio summer she was used to. She knew it would still get hot here in Maine, but the ocean breeze was really pleasant.

They found the town square and the library without any difficulty. Reagan applied for a library card and checked out several books. When she filled out her address, the librarian looked at her steadily for a few seconds. Reagan mentioned that she was staying with her Aunt Willow for the summer, and the librarian seemed satisfied, but she shook her head and tsked a couple of times. Reagan looked at her, confused, and Becky spoke up.

"Is there a problem?"

"No, of course not," the librarian replied. "Willow James just doesn't seem the type to tolerate having a teenager around." Becky raised an eyebrow at the comment. "She's very nice," the librarian added, hastily. "She's lived alone for so long, it's hard to imagine…" her voice drifted off. "Well, here you go," she said as she handed over the stack of books. "Remember, these are due in two weeks." She was brisk and efficient, dismissing the two of them as she turned to gather a stack of returned items.

Reagan and her mom looked at each other, and Reagan shrugged. "I've got to say, Mom, this place is a lot weird. Not only is Aunt Willow weird, but this whole town seems like something out of a Stephen King book. It's a good thing I don't get into that sort of thing." She looked down at the stack of crime mysteries she had checked out.

"People in small towns are very protective and wary of strangers, and the librarian is right, your aunt has been alone for a long time. I just want you to know she didn't even hesitate when I asked if you could stay. I won't say she gushed about it, but she was very matter-of-fact that you were welcome. My guess is that you will be left to your own devices. Now put those books in the car and let's check out the square."

They walked the quaint square, looking into the shop windows. They agreed that it was like a page out of the past. The windows were mullioned, like Willow's house. There was an attorney's office, a bakery, a drug store, a small diner, and an old-fashioned hardware store. The city offices were also located on the square next to the library. They found the pizza place in one corner, quietly displaying a sign that stated that Antonio's not only had pizza, but delicious pastas, calzones, salads, and cannoli's. The smell coming from the shop was unexpectedly delectable.

Smiling with appreciation, they went in and ordered two medium pizzas. Realizing they had no idea what kind of pizza Aunt Willow would like, they ordered a deluxe and a vegetarian. While they waited for the pizzas, they sat at a table near a window, watching for any sign of interesting activity. The town was dead.

"There is no one out there," said Reagan. "There isn't a kid or a teenager anywhere in sight. I may have to get a lot more books." She sighed, but then caught the look on her mom's face. "I know I was a pain in the butt earlier, and I'm sorry. I will make the best of it. You know I love to read, so this is the summer I get to relax and read to my heart's content. It's all good." They looked out on the empty square until the food was ready and then drove back to Willow's, the car filled with the heady aroma of hot pizza.

Willow was just coming out of the barn when Reagan and her mom drove in with dinner. Wiley came running up, happily wagging his tail. He no longer considered them a threat.

"Please tell me you got some meat on that pizza," said Willow as she approached the car. "I don't want you to think my hippie persona extends to a vegetarian existence."

"We weren't sure, so we got a deluxe and a vegetarian," said Becky, trying to reassure Willow that they weren't stereotyping her.

"I'll eat just about anything, but I do like pepperoni, and Wiley here will eat any kind of pizza bones you offer him."

"Pizza bones?" questioned Reagan

"The crusts," said Becky and Willow together.

"Your father always called them that," said Willow wistfully. "He was always slipping his dog the crusts."

"Wait, I didn't know Dad had a dog," said Reagan.

"Really?" Willow looked sideways at Reagan as they walked to the house. "He had a collie named Scout. He adored that dog. They went everywhere together. That dog never left his side. When Scout died, I think a piece of your dad died with him. It was one of the saddest days I can remember, a real tragedy."

"What happened?"

"I'll tell you over pizza. I'm hungry," said Willow as she opened the door to the kitchen, letting Becky pass through with the two aromatic boxes.

They settled at the large kitchen table. Willow grabbed a handful of paper plates and threw them on the table. Reagan looked for napkins, but Willow gestured at the roll of paper towels. Shrugging, Reagan picked up the roll and set it on the table while her mom grabbed some cans of Pepsi out of the fridge.

"So, tell me about my dad's dog," inquired Reagan as she nibbled on a piece of vegetarian pizza. She was shocked at how good it was. Who knew this backwoods hick town could have pizza this good?

"Scout was just about the best dog that walked the earth," Willow started. "He was dedicated to all of us, and fiercely protective. Your father picked him from a litter from Roger Whitstock, down the road a piece. He's an old man now and still can raise really fine collies. Your dad had wanted one of Whitstock's pups for a long time, but Wolf had to save his money. Mom and Dad didn't have the cash for a purebred. They offered to take Wolf to the county kennel to rescue a dog. In fact, they would have preferred that, but your dad wanted a Whitstock collie. He saved for two years or so, working his paper route every day and not buying himself anything during that time. The rest of us would go to the movies or get a malt from the drugstore, but not your dad. He wanted that dog. Sometimes I would pay for his way into the theater and get him a malt. After all, I owed him…" Willow grabbed another piece of deluxe pizza.

"Why did you owe him?" asked Becky.

"That's not important," said Willow, waving away the comment with impatience. She was warming to the story, and she didn't want to be interrupted. Reagan had just about finished her first piece of pizza when she felt a wet nose push firmly into her hand. She looked under the table and the liquid brown eyes of Wiley gazed up at her. A string of drool hung from the black flappy stuff on the side of his lower jaw. Reagan glanced at Willow and leaned down to slip him a 'bone'. Willow nodded her permission.

"Anyway, after saving up all of his money, he contacted Whitstock. Your dad knew one of Whitstock's bitches was going to drop a litter soon, and he wanted the pick. Whitstock took a deposit, and your dad waited for that day. When the time came, your dad selected a male pup and named him Scout. Then, when it was time for the pup to be separated from his mother, Wolf walked to Whitstock's farm and then carried that pup in his arms as he walked the four miles home. They were inseparable."

"One day, when Scout was four years old or so, he and your dad were down on the rocks on the beach. No one really knows what happened that day, but your dad ended up in the surf. Probably a rogue wave. There are strong currents down there, and your dad was being swept out to sea. It was November and very cold. Scout went crazy, barking and running back and forth. When he realized your dad wasn't going to make it to shore, he jumped in and tried to bring him to safety. Now collies are herding dogs. It was his instinct to save your dad, but collies are not water dogs. Wiley here is a Lab." Wiley's tail thumped the floor as he recognized his name. "He would have had no trouble bringing Wolf in, but Scout, not so much luck. Long story short, Scout was able to bring your dad out of the surf, but he died in the process."

Becky looked startled. She had never heard this story from her husband.

"Wolf never told you about it, did he?" asked Willow. "I'm not surprised. He never really talked to anyone about it after it happened. After that, your dad couldn't wait to leave this place. That's all he talked about, and once he did leave, he never came back. Never set his foot here again." Willow looked sad as she said that, but then she reached for a piece of the vegetarian pizza. "Just as well, he wouldn't have been happy coming back, and I hated to see him unhappy."

"How old was my dad when Scout died?" asked Reagan.

"He was seventeen."

"Wow, I figured he was younger," said Reagan. "You mean at seventeen, he couldn't swim back?"

"Nope. I think that's one of the things that really bothered him. He figured it was his fault that Scout died. He was old enough to not do something so stupid as to fall in when the ocean surf was pounding like that. It was even low tide, but something must have gone wrong. Like I said, he wouldn't talk about it, and I stopped asking him. Especially when he kept trying to get me to move away from here. He refused to come back, and I refused to leave. This is my home, complete with my memories and ghosts."

"That's so weird that Wolf never told me about any of that, but to be honest, he really never talked about his home. He talked about you a lot. I know that he adored you. He loved those evenings when you guys would talk for hours on the phone, but he never even offered to bring me here," said Becky.

"Mom, you never came here? But you met Aunt Willow before, right?" said Reagan.

"I met your Aunt Willow when she came to Cleveland for a gallery opening. Her pottery was featured at one of the galleries in the Cleveland area, so she stayed with us for a few days. That was when you were just a baby. Then she visited a couple more times when she had some more shows in the area, but it's been years."

"Why didn't you come to Cleveland anymore?" asked Reagan.

"I don't like to travel that much, and I decided to concentrate on showing here on the East Coast. Later on, I was able to sell all over the country through my website, so there wasn't any need to travel. I'm busy enough as it is, so I didn't have to."

"Well, I'm sorry that we fell out of touch," said Becky, "and I wish that we could visit more, but I have to catch a flight in the morning, and then I will have a long day getting briefed and settling in for my assignment. Reagan, we need to leave here at 6:30 in the morning, so be sure that you set your alarm to get up in time to drive me to the airport. Good night, sweetie. Good-night, Willow." Becky absently pat Wiley on the head as she walked past him on the way to the garbage can. He slithered a slimy tongue over the back of her wrist. Reagan laughed at the expression on her mom's face.

"I don't think Mom is much of a dog person," said Reagan.

"No doubt," agreed Willow. "I have some work to do in my office, so I assume you can fend for yourself. Right? If you need anything, just nose around. I'm sure you'll find it. Don't be surprised if Wiley joins you in the middle of the night. He wanders around the house keeping guard. He sleeps wherever the mood takes him. By the way," said Willow on her way out of the room, "which bedroom did you choose?"

"The cornflower blue room that faces the ocean. Is that okay?"

"Good choice. It's Adelaide's room. I'm sure she won't mind." With that Willow walked out of the kitchen, walked down the front hall and closed herself into her office leaving Reagan standing in the kitchen with her mouth hanging open.

Who the hell is Adelaide, thought Reagan as she cleaned up the mess on the table. What did Willow mean when she said it was Adelaide's room, and she wouldn't mind? Was someone else living there? But the room was completely empty when Reagan moved her things in. In fact, all the rooms were empty. The only one that looked lived in was the one in the servants' hall that her mom had guessed was Aunt Willow's. And why was Aunt Willow so damned cryptic?

Reagan's head was hurting, and she was tired. Maybe she heard her aunt wrong, but she was just too whipped to puzzle it out. Satisfied that the kitchen was clean, she turned out the light and headed up to her room.

Popping her head in her mom's room, she said her goodnights. Then she turned down her own bed and snatched up her toiletry kit. The shared bathroom was down the hall. As she brushed her teeth, she thought she would like to snuggle in bed and read for a bit before she turned out her light for good. Damn, she thought. She left her library books out in the car. Sighing, she headed downstairs again and opened the door to go outside. Wiley shot between her legs and stood in front of her on the porch.

"What's the matter, buddy? You're in my way. I need to go to the car to get my books. Why am I talking out loud to a dog?" She pushed past him and stepped off the porch. Wiley growled a low, throaty growl. At first Reagan thought he was growling at her, but then she realized he was staring into the darkness off to the right of the porch.

"Why are you growling? Is there something out there?" A tendril of fear curled its way through Reagan's gut. Another growl and a low bark. Reagan peered into the darkness. She wasn't used to it being so dark at night. In the subdivision where she lived, there was a streetlight every fifth driveway, lighting up the sidewalks and giving the front lawns a soft glow. Here, at Aunt Willow's, the world was a lot different.

A light fog from the ocean was swirling over the cliffs. A half-moon lit the sky, making eerie shadows in the fog. The screen door slammed behind her making her jump, terrified.

"What are you doing out here in the dark?" asked Willow, quietly.

"I forgot my library books in the car. I wanted to grab them so that I could read a little."

"It's not a good idea to go wandering around here at night. It's not safe."

"What do you mean it's not safe? It's not like the bogey man is going to get me," retorted Reagan a little too shrilly, her fear showing through her bravado.

"No, probably not, but there are cliffs you can't see in the dark, and the night animals will be out. You wouldn't want to run into a skunk at night, would you?" asked Willow, "although that would be a hell of a lot better than running into the bogey man, don't you think? Now go ahead and run to your car for your books. Wiley, go with her." The dog whined softly. "Wiley, go, protect."

Reagan looked at her aunt and decided right then and there that the woman was crazy. Squaring her shoulders and banishing all stupid thoughts of scary things, Reagan boldly strode to the car, grabbed her books, and came back to the porch. Wiley stuck to her leg the entire way. When she reached the porch, Reagan smiled sweetly at her aunt, told her goodnight, and flounced upstairs to her room, muttering under her breath the whole way that she was stuck for the summer with a certifiable aunt.

CHAPTER 5

*B*eep. Beep. Beep. Reagan's alarm insistently continued to ring, while Reagan consistently ignored it. She rolled to her right side and was surprised by a sloppy tongue slathering her face with spit. Ugh, she thought. I don't know if I will ever get used to that. Despite her disgust, she reached her hand out from under the covers to scratch Wiley behind the ear.

"Reagan, are you getting up?" her mother called.

"Yep, I'm jumping in the shower right now," Reagan lied as she snuggled further down into the bed.

"Reagan, we are in a place with only one bathroom between us, and I am currently in it, so, no, you are not jumping in the shower right now."

"In my mind I am already halfway done showering. Besides, I obviously can't shower if you are in there." Smiling at the thought of outwitting her mom, Reagan closed her eyes for a snooze.

"If you don't want me to park my car in a rental lot for the summer where you can't have access to it, I suggest you get your butt in that shower now. And make it a three-minute shower at that." Recognizing the seriousness of the threat, Reagan reluctantly crawled out of bed. The room was brisk from leaving the windows open all night, but she'd slept like a baby. The sun was streaming through the lace curtains and the pretty room was cheerful. Maybe this summer isn't going to be so bad. Maybe Aunt Willow really isn't crazy. Maybe she's just messing with me. Floating on the remarkably good mood that she woke up in, Reagan readied herself to take her mom to the airport. Despite the fact that she was going to miss her mom, and she was very sad to see her go, Reagan had decided that she was going to make the best of her situation. As soon as she got back from dropping off her mom she was going to explore the beach and the rest of her new domain.

Reagan felt a gnawing emptiness in the pit of her stomach when she returned from the airport, but she was determined to make the best out of her situation. Becky cried when they'd said goodbye, and that made Reagan feel terrible. She knew this was harder on her mom than it was on her. After all, not only was her mom going to miss her, but Becky also felt guilty for having to leave her. Mom was getting hit with a double whammy. At least Becky was going to be doing a job that would take all of her concentration so she would be occupied most of the time. Reagan hoped that would help ease some of Becky's pain.

She parked the car onto the gravel pad in front of the barn, Reagan stepped out of the car and looked around for Wiley. He was nowhere to be seen. She felt disappointed because she was counting on him to go exploring with her. She wanted to drop her purse in the house and change into her running shoes before she tackled the cliffs, so she ran up the porch stairs and burst into the kitchen, thinking about the adventure ahead.

She was startled by the smell of freshly baked cinnamon rolls and the sight of a skinny older woman with deeply tanned, wrinkled arms, a sharp hook nose, and stringy salt and pepper hair pulled back in a severe pony tail.

"Oh, um, sorry, I'm..."

"You must be Wolf's girl," the woman stated flatly. "I'm Cora Rose. Have a cinnamon roll." She didn't say it invitingly in the least bit. "Go ahead, get a plate off the sideboard and have a cinnamon roll. You're too skinny as it is."

This place was getting weirder by the minute. Reagan looked at the sideboard to see a bowl of scrambled eggs, slices of fried ham, and a pan of gooey, iced cinnamon rolls.

"You can have some breakfast, too, but eat the damn roll while it's hot. It's best that way." Cora Rose abruptly turned her back on Reagan and began to wash the dishes that were piled in the sink; a testament to the trouble she had gone through to make breakfast.

"I see you've met Cora Rose," said Aunt Willow as she came down the hall from her office. "She is always a bright fixture to start my morning."

"Humph," was the only reply from the strange woman.

"Eat some breakfast," said Willow, "or Cora Rose might have a coronary, and then who would clean my house and make me my favorite meal of the day? We do everything we can to keep Cora Rose happy."

"You know I am right here and can hear you," groused Cora Rose.

"I expect you can." Willow grabbed a plate and piled it high with fluffy eggs and browned slices of ham. Reagan's stomach growled at the tantalizing odors.

"I usually only have a cup of coffee in the morning," protested Reagan. Willow and Cora Rose shared a glance.

"That needs to change. Get a plate," insisted Willow. "Cora Rose cooks a big breakfast every morning, and that's the last thing she makes. Then she goes about her business of cleaning my house. She leaves by 11:00. I don't do lunch, and then usually only a light dinner. It would behoove you to tuck away considerable food in the morning to get you through the day. Besides, it's healthier to eat in the morning."

"Now I have to make coffee every morning, too. Why can't you drink Pepsi like your aunt?" Shocked, Reagan glanced at the table where two places were set. At one, a can of Pepsi was waiting. Cora Rose was in the process of placing an empty mug at the other place. "It'll take a minute for the coffee, so you'll just have to wait."

"I wasn't complaining," protested Reagan, "I just meant that I didn't need you to do anything special for me." Reagan caught the amused look on Willow's face as if she was thoroughly enjoying Reagan's discomfort.

Reagan dutifully picked up a plate and filled it with a small serving of everything on the sideboard and took her place at the table. Cora Rose slapped a steaming cup of coffee in front of her and raised one eyebrow. "Cream and sugar, I suppose."

"Yes, please," Reagan said meekly. Willow burst out laughing.

"You're going to have to grow a thicker skin than that if you are going to survive around here. Now dig in." Reagan tasted a forkful of eggs. Amazing. They were absolutely delicious.

"Let me guess," Cora Rose said, "you've never had fresh, free range eggs before, have you?" Reagan shook her head no. "Figures," Cora Rose complained

"Cora has chickens, and not only does she cook us breakfast, she supplies our eggs. Try the ham. It's pretty damn delicious, too."

Reagan dug in with a lot more enthusiasm than she expected. The food was wonderful, and the cinnamon rolls were heavenly. Cora Rose looked satisfied when she swiped away Reagan's plate. "Coffee okay?" Cora Rose asked, expectedly.

"Yes, delicious. I like it strong like this."

"Good, it's the only way to drink it."

"Reagan, I have to work on a large order of bowls today. What do you plan on doing?" asked Willow

"I figured I would do some exploring," said Reagan

Both Willow and Cora Rose's heads snapped up in unison, and they held each other's eyes for a split second.

"Where do you plan on exploring?" asked Willow, mildly.

"I saw a path from my window that looks like it leads down the cliffs to the beach. I thought I would start there."

"There is a path, and it will take you down to the ocean. There isn't much of a beach. It's more of a rocky shoreline. When the tide is out, you have some area you can walk, and there are some nice tidal pools in the rocks. When the tide is in, you can just pass along the cliff on the high rocks. The ocean is pretty quiet today, so you won't have to worry too much. Just stay out of the water. This is not the place to go swimming. If you want to do that, you will have to head south of town to Orchard Bend. There is a swimming beach there. When you're done exploring there, you can check out the old gardens and the back fields. That should take most of the afternoon. Please, just let me know when you come back up the cliff, and take Wiley with you."

"Where is Wiley?" asked Reagan. As if on cue, Wiley whined at the porch screen door. Reagan got up and let the dog in.

"He was out for his morning constitutional. Lord knows where he was, or what he was getting into. Okay, I am heading out to work. Be careful with your exploring. Also, make yourself at home in here."

"As long as you stay off the fourth floor," snapped Cora Rose. Willow shot her a warning look.

"I already told Reagan she is not welcome up there and that it is dangerous. No need to make a big deal of it, Cora Rose," said Willow, sharply. Cora Rose stared Willow down and then turned around and stomped out of the kitchen, mumbling something about added laundry duties with the additional house guest.

"Well, unless you need anything, I will see you later." With that,

Willow grabbed another Pepsi out of the refrigerator and headed out the door.

"Wiley, is everyone here bat-shit crazy or what?" complained Reagan. "And what the hell is the problem with the fourth floor?" The dog stood stock still and growled softly. "Great, you're nuts, too."

CHAPTER 6

*R*eagan skipped down the front porch steps, suddenly feeling happy to be alive. The ocean air felt salty, almost sticky against her skin, but not unpleasant. Pausing as she passed the barn, she listened to see if she could hear anything coming from the studio where her aunt worked. She wondered if she would ever be invited in to see what a potter's studio looked like. Wiley pushed her forward with his nose and led the way past the barn into the back meadow. He nosed his way along a path through tall grasses, pausing to snap at a butterfly or two. Reagan couldn't help but smile. She never had a dog, actually never really thought about wanting a dog, but she was glad Wiley was here with her. She could get used to this. Wondering if her mom would let her get a dog when they got home, she worked her way to the edge of the cliff where the path turned and led down the steep rocks to the ocean below. The sky was blue, and the ocean was gray. Gentle waves slapped against the rocks while sea gulls whirled overhead. Wiley looked at her expectantly, then disappeared behind the wall of the cliff as he headed down the path.

Reagan followed, carefully stepping, a little unnerved by the steep and narrow path. She finally reached the bottom and came to the sinking realization that she would have to climb back up. Turning to look down the beach, she was stunned of the lack of sand. She had been to the ocean before. Her mom had taken her to Ocean City, Maryland a couple of years ago. They had a wonderful time sunning themselves on the warm beach, flying kites in the brisk on-shore breeze, and eating crabs at night on the boardwalk. But this was different. Completely different. There was very little sand, and what there was of it was nestled between large rocks that looked very slippery.

She left the path cautiously and stood on a large slab of stone that sloped toward the water. Waves crashed over the end of the slab, sending a spray of water into the air. Wiley ran through the waves, barking and biting at the sea foam. Reagan laughed at the dog's crazy antics. Finding a relatively dry spot, she settled herself to watch the dog and the crashing waves.

The longer she sat, the more she became aware of her surroundings. Next to her on the rock was a puddle of water. She had noticed it when she sat down, being careful not to land her butt in it, but when she glanced at again, she realized it was kind of deep, and that there were things in it. She leaned over to get a closer look and was startled to discover a starfish slowly moving across the rock. She had never seen a live starfish before, just the skeletons of them in craft stores. Fascinated, she looked closer. In the puddle was what looked like algae, and even some kind of plant, maybe seaweed. A tiny crab scuttled by. Then she saw something like a spiny ball.

"What the hell is that?" she said out loud.

"A sea urchin."

Startled, Reagan almost fell backward on the rock.

"Sorry, I didn't mean to scare you," said the boy who was standing next to her.

"Where did you come from, and who are you?" asked Reagan.

"I came from over there," he gestured vaguely behind him.

Reagan looked, but only saw the curve of the cliff and rocks. "And my name is Seth."

"Well, Seth, you really shouldn't sneak up on people like that," said Reagan, trying to cover up her embarrassment with indignation. The boy just laughed and continued to stare down at her.

"You really shouldn't be so involved in something that you don't notice someone approach you. It might not be safe."

When he said that, Reagan felt a chill down her spine. She couldn't put her finger on it, but there was something really not quite right about this boy. She squinted up at him, the sun behind him making it hard to see his face. His blond hair was the color of straw. It was long and windblown as if he had already been on the shore for a long time this morning. He was wearing some blue cotton type pants and a white button up shirt, untucked and somewhat wrinkled. If she were to venture a guess, she would say he was a local, because a tourist would be dressed in all the latest fashions. This guy looked like he may have shopped at the local Goodwill, trying to pick up some vintage clothes. Perhaps this was Maine's nod to the counter culture like the Goth movement back home.

Wiley didn't seem to think the kid was a threat, because he came bounding out of the water, hurling himself at the boy, butt wiggling, tail wagging, and whining with happiness. Thinking that she may have been too quick to judge, and a bit rude, she softened her tone,

"You two seem to know each other," she said.

"We've run into each other a time or two, haven't we boy?" Wiley just groaned in pleasure as Seth rubbed the dog's back at the base of his tail. "So, you've never seen a sea urchin?" asked Seth.

"No, I haven't. It looks like a porcupine," said Reagan

"More like a hedgehog."

"Well, I've never seen one of those, either."

"But you've seen a porcupine?"

"Well, no... wait, yes, in the zoo," exclaimed Reagan, triumphantly

"Well, these guys are related to the starfish, and they are good eating," said Seth.

"Wait, you eat these spiny things?"

"Yep, you can eat the urchin, but a lot of people just like the eggs," said Seth. Reagan wrinkled her nose. She was an Ohio girl. Seafood was shrimp, crabs, fish, and maybe some sushi for the adventurous crowd, of which she was not.

"So, is he or she trapped here? Should we try to get the starfish and this urchin back into the ocean?"

"Where are you from?" asked Seth

"Ohio, why?"

"Because you don't know that you are looking at a tidal pool. Who doesn't know what a tidal pool is?"

"A girl from Ohio, that's who. We don't have an ocean there," Reagan replied hotly.

"I'm sorry," said Seth as he crouched down beside her. "I didn't want to make you mad. I was just surprised that's all. So, when the tide is high, these rocks are under water. When the tide goes out, these pools form in the rocks. The animals will be fine here until the water covers them up again when the tide rises."

"That makes sense," said Reagan, suddenly smiling at him.

"What? Why are you smiling?" asked Seth, a little nervously.

"Because I haven't seen anyone my age around here since I got here, but you're living proof that there are others. Maybe my summer won't be so lonely after all." Her declaration was cut short by a shrill scream that ended abruptly. Wiley stiffened and growled, looking up at the cliff, and Seth stood up. "What the hell was that?" asked Reagan.

"It was nothing," said Seth.

"I heard a scream," said Reagan, rising to her feet. "It sounded weird, like it was over by the cliff, but there isn't anyone here."

"Nah, it was just the wind. Sometimes it whistles through the rocks. It can really spook you if you let your imagination run away with you." Seth started scratching Wiley's fur again, and the dog relaxed. "Well, I have to go. It was nice meeting you, Reagan." He turned and walked quickly in the direction he had gestured toward earlier, disappearing around the cliff remarkably quickly.

"Nice meeting you, too," Reagan called after him, although for the life of her, she swore she never told him her name.

Reagan spent the rest of the afternoon parked on the porch swing reading one of the detective novels she had picked up at the library. She was addicted to them. Given the opportunity, she could spend an entire day and well into an evening reading a book straight through. At home she never got the chance to do that because she was always running around with one of her friends. Maybe staying at Aunt Willow's wasn't going to be so bad. Her aunt obviously didn't have an agenda for Reagan, so she was free to do whatever her little heart desired and being lazy all day reading was right up her alley. She didn't even notice that the shadows were getting longer, and the day was beginning to chill down until she heard her aunt's footsteps on the wooden steps.

"I used to spend the day reading myself. Not a bad way to pass the time." She plopped her ample body down into a rocking chair with a sigh. Reagan glanced over at her aunt. Her hands were damp, as though she washed them quickly, with specks of clay still clinging to her wrists. Her t-shirt had a line of splattered muddy streaks across the belly, and pieces of her long graying hair had slipped from the single braid that laid down her back. She looked tired.

"Did you have a good day, Aunt Willow?" Reagan asked.

Willow looked surprised at the question, as if no one had ever asked her that before. She considered before answering.

"Yes, I did. I had a large order of graduated matching serving bowls that I needed to get done for a New York caterer. I finished throwing the last one today."

"Throwing?"

"Yes, throwing," said Willow, laughing. "That's what it is called when you make things on a wheel. Some potters call it turning, but I use the older term. Now the pots need to air dry. Once they are completely dry, I will fire them in the kiln for the first time. That's the bisque firing. After that, I make sure everything is perfect, getting rid of any rough spots or bumps, and then I glaze them and fire them again. I give them one final inspection, then pack them and ship them, praying they get to their destination in one piece."

"That sounds really cool. Can I watch you someday?" asked Reagan. Willow hesitated, thinking.

"Maybe. I don't do well sharing my private space, my creative space... but we'll see."

"I'm sorry. I didn't mean to intrude..." said Reagan, somewhat embarrassed.

"No, you're not intruding. It's good you're curious. Look, I've been alone for a long time. A very long time. Cora Rose is the only person I see on a regular basis. I have never been good with people. Don't get me wrong. I'm glad you're here. I'm glad I could help out your mom, just don't expect me to be a good conversationalist or a best friend, because I've never been very good at that."

"I understand. I always have lots of friends around, so I might not be too good at being alone. I'll try not to get on your nerves, and I will respect the fact that you are not ready to let me into your inner sanctum. Okay?"

"Sounds like a plan. Are you hungry? Did your breakfast wear off yet?" Willow asked with a grin.

"Actually, no. It's like I won't ever need to eat again," laughed Reagan.

"That's the whole idea. I usually have a snack or a sandwich in the evening, but I don't want you to suffer nutritionally, so is there anything you need or that I should get you?"

"No, but a sandwich or maybe a salad later would be good. If you need me to, I can always go to town to get groceries or whatever we need," Reagan offered.

"That's not necessary. All you need to do is to put what you want on the grocery list that is hanging on the side of the fridge. Cora Rose will pick up whatever groceries we need on the next trip, so if there's something special, just write it down. We usually have a couple of different types of lunch meat and cheeses, and there is always bread. I don't generally have a salad, but there should be plenty of things to make one since I put lettuce and tomatoes on my sandwiches. Just check the fridge when you go in and add salad stuff to the list."

"Okay, but I would like to carry my own weight here. If there is anything I can do, please let me know."

"Okay. Now I'm going to go in and clean up. Make sure you come in before it gets dark, and please remember to lock the door. Bring Wiley with you."

"Will do." Willow stiffly rose from the rocker and went into the house. Wiley raised his head and watched her go but was content to remain next to Reagan. Yep, Reagan really liked having a dog around.

CHAPTER 7

*W*iley stood up, hackles raised, and stared into the night. Reagan had fallen asleep reading in the rocking chair. She had shared a sandwich with Willow and then came back out on the porch to finish her book. When Willow disappeared into the office, she reminded Reagan to be sure to come in before dark and to lock the door. Falling asleep was not something Reagan had planned to do. Now, she was stiff and chilly. A mosquito was currently gorging itself on her bare forearm, and something was making Wiley extremely uneasy. He growled softly and moved his body protectively against Reagan's leg. He tensed even more. Reagan stood, peering off the porch into the darkness. Wiley whimpered.

"Is anyone out there?" she asked. Stupid, she thought to herself. If someone was out there, I would know, and Wiley would be running at them barking. This is like all those stupid horror movies where the dumb teen asks who's out there. I'm the dumb teen. Except this isn't a movie, and there is no bogey man. Reagan reached over to pick up her fallen book when Wiley lurched forward with a snarl and a snap. At the same moment Reagan felt an ice-cold touch envelop her. It was like the door had opened to winter. She gasped, and Wiley began growling and snapping wildly. Then she heard it. A voice. A voice that said, "go home." What the hell? Wiley whimpered then stopped barking. The cold dissipated, and Wiley relaxed.

Walking quickly, Reagan pulled open the kitchen door and hurried inside, bringing Wiley with her. She locked the door and shot the deadbolt. Unnerved, she stood in the bright light of the kitchen's overhead light. Did that just happen? What the heck was that? She reached down and patted Wiley's head. He happily wagged his tail as if nothing at all had happened. Had it? Was she just still groggy from sleeping awkwardly in a chair? It was just remnants of a dream, she told herself. Don't be silly. She shook herself and laughed. Wow, her imagination was running away from her. She snapped off the kitchen light and headed upstairs to her room

As Reagan climbed the stairs, she heard the faint sound of singing, a sweet female voice singing what sounded like an old-fashioned folk-song. Reagan paused, straining her ears to figure out where it was coming from. The sound swirled faintly in the large central stairwell opening. She continued climbing, and for a moment, it sounded like it was coming from her bedroom, but then it abruptly stopped. Maybe her aunt was listening to the radio or something. She put her now finished book on one side of the small desk in her room and selected another to start in the morning. Taking a minute, she sat at the dressing table and brushed her hair out until it shone. Looking at her reflection in the mirror, she smiled to see that the tip of her nose and cheek-bones were slightly sunburned, the result of her morning on the beach.

Finishing, she lay her brush down and lined up her small bottle of perfume, hand lotion, and hand mirror. She laughed at herself and her neat freak tendencies. Here of all places, she didn't need to make sure her things were just so, her aunt couldn't care less, but Reagan hated things that were out of place, so before bed, she always straightened her room. Not that there is much here to straighten, she thought. Climbing into the big antique bed, Reagan sighed. She was worn out. In minutes, she had slipped into a deep sleep.

Something was stroking her face, her forehead, a soft touch. A gentle touch. Fleeting, like a curtain in the wind, brushing, tickling, but resilient, like flesh. A familiar smell reached her nose. Light and floral. Then, nothing. Reagan rolled over in her sleep.

Morning streamed in through the open windows. Songbirds greeted the day with blissful happiness. Reagan stretched, luxuriating in her bed, letting the last vestige of sleep slip away like a dream ...

She had a dream last night. Someone was here with her. A friend, lightly touching her forehead. It felt familiar, like it was a touch she knew. She smiled. She liked dreams when they weren't scary. This one left her feeling loved and cared for. That was nice. What else was nice was the smell of coffee wafting up the stairs. It smelled amazing.

She swung her feet to the floor, her toes recoiling at the chill of the hardwood. Grabbing her robe, she slipped it on and sat in front of the mirror. She felt a little silly and a little like a princess. She never had a dressing table with a mirror before, and she felt a little like the Barbies she used to play with. Barbie had all of those things.

Absently, she reached for her hairbrush, but it wasn't there. That's strange. She distinctly remembered straightening up the dressing table before she went to bed and yet her brush was missing, and the top was off of her perfume. What the hell? She stood up and turned around. There, on top of the dresser was her brush. Had she accidentally left it there last night? Had she walked around brushing her hair? No, she was sure she hadn't, and she sure as hell hadn't use any perfume last night.

Retrieving her brush, she swiped it through her hair and carefully placed it on the dressing table next to the bottle of perfume. She put the cap on the spray bottle firmly. Checking once again to make sure everything was where it belonged, she left the room, walking down the hall to the bathroom to shower.

Helping herself to a cup of coffee on the sideboard, Reagan casually mentioned the moved hairbrush and the lid that had been pulled off the perfume bottle.

"I can't understand what could have happened. You guys didn't come into my room or anything last night or early this morning, did you?" asked Reagan, shyly. Willow and Cora Rose exchanged glances. The look wasn't lost on Reagan. "What's going on? Did one of you move my stuff?" Her voice was pitching higher than usual.

"No dear," said Willow. "Neither one of us was in your room. We would have no reason to. Cora Rose will go up to clean during the day and to change sheets, but not during the night. Are you sure you put everything back where you think you did? Maybe you were tired, and you just don't remember."

"Maybe you sleepwalk," said Cora Rose rudely.

"I've never sleepwalked in my life," Reagan retorted.

"There's always a first time," Cora Rose came back.

"Be nice," warned Willow, giving Cora Rose a significant glare.

"Well, either she went to sleepwalking, or a ghost moved them. Take your pick," countered Cora Rose. Reagan nearly blew hot coffee out her nose as she snorted with laughter.

"I'm sure it was a ghost," said Reagan sarcastically. "She liked my perfume and needed to brush her rotting tresses."

"Humph," grumbled Cora Rose, "you'll see. Wait until you see the eyes of the wolves. That will convince you."

"The eyes of the wolves?" asked Reagan, getting drawn into the drama.

"Sure. They live under the dining room table. Sometimes you can see them at night." Again, Reagan burst out laughing. Willow looked amused, and Cora Rose looked pissed. Again, Willow shot her a warning look.

"Cora Rose has a bit of an imagination," soothed Willow. "Sometimes it runs away with her."

"Did your grandmother have a bit of an imagination when she was bitten under that same dining room table? Did Adelaide have a bit of imagination when she was dragged down the cellar stairs?"

"Cora Rose, enough! Stop carrying tales. I won't tolerate it," Willow reprimanded her sharply. Cora Rose glowered at Willow and started to say something else but stopped herself. She tossed a plate of waffles on the sideboard and left the room in a huff.

"I'm sorry, Reagan. The locals here are a superstitious crowd. If they don't understand something, they make it up. I'm sure there is a logical explanation for your brush being moved. Perhaps you did get up in the night, but you don't remember. You are still settling into a strange, old house. It might just take some getting used to. So, are you okay? I was getting ready to head out to the barn to work."

"No, I'm fine, thank you. I am going to run into town to get a few things today that I need. Can I get you anything or do anything for you?" asked Reagan.

"Thank you, but no. Have a good afternoon." With that Willow walked out the door. Reagan put her coffee on the table and loaded her plate with some waffles and breakfast sausage links. If she kept eating like this, she was going to have to take up running. As she munched on a waffle, the exchange between Aunt Willow and Cora Rose rewound through her head. Something Cora Rose said bothered her, other than that whole craziness of the wolves under the dining room table thing. What the heck was it?

Adelaide. That's what it was. She said that Adelaide was dragged down the cellar stairs. Wasn't that the name Willow said when Reagan mentioned she had picked the cornflower blue room? Didn't she say that the room was Adelaide's and that she wouldn't mind? Who the heck was Adelaide?

CHAPTER 8

*R*eagan left the drugstore with her purchases in a small bag. She headed toward the car intending to go home and read for a little while and then take a walk down the cliff. Maybe she would even read sitting on the rocks at the shore. As she unlocked her car, she glanced up and noticed the small diner on the corner. A sign in the window touted the fact that they made "famous chocolate malts." Grinning, she decided to treat herself. She tossed her purchases in the car, locked it again, and headed over to the diner.

The Corner Grill looked like a local teen hangout that hadn't seen an update in many, many years. The "retro style" had already gone in and out of fashion many times over the years. Reagan settled herself at the counter and absently looked at the menu. She wasn't hungry after her large breakfast, but she was curious as to the choices should she ever decide to get a bite when in town. It was typical dinner fare, complete with meatloaf, fried chicken, and clam strips. The pies and cakes in the cases looked fresh and delicious, and the smell of onion rings was heady.

A grandmotherly lady took her order for a chocolate malt and waddled off to the big silver mixer to make it. As Reagan was watching the waitress drop huge scoopfuls of ice cream into the silver tumbler, she became aware of a conversation in hushed voices being carried on behind her.

"That must be the girl who is staying at Willow James' place. I heard it is her niece."

"What kind of mom would drop her kid off at a place like that? She has to be nuts."

"Shh, guys, be nice. She might hear us."

The waitress plopped a napkin and a place mat down in front of Reagan. She filled a frosted, tall mug to the top with malt and left the tumbler on the counter next to the mug. When Reagan peered into the tumbler, she saw that there was still a third of the shake left. This was going to take a while.

She slowly spun around on her stool while taking a draw on her straw, working the thick malt up into her mouth. She leveled a stare at the group of teenagers who were still contemplating her existence. One of the girls noticed and kicked the boy sitting next to her into silence.

Reagan slowly slid off her stool and ambled up to the kids, sucking down the malt the whole time.

"Yep, I am the girl who is living at Willow James' house. My name is Reagan, and my mother is not nuts. In fact, my mother is currently on an assignment covering our soldiers in Afghanistan, so I am hanging out at my aunt's house. Is that okay with you guys?" A redheaded, freckle-faced beauty rolled her eyes a bit, but had the decency to look away after that. The young man's face blushed slightly, and then he scowled. The third girl, a pretty brunette with an open, honest face was the only one who spoke.

"I'm sorry. We were rude."

Then the redhead spoke up, emboldened. "It's just that no one goes out there if they know what's good for them. That place is haunted. Everybody knows that."

"Oh yeah?" said Reagan. "I haven't seen any ghosts. What makes you think it's haunted?"

"My grandma told me a story about a boy who died out there. It was really weird. He was down at the ocean one day. Somehow, he fell in. My grandma says that his dog tried to rescue him. You know, like drag him out of the water, but he couldn't. The kid disappeared under the waves. They say he drowned, but no one ever found the body. Well, that's what everyone said, but my grandma said that some fisherman saw a body on the rocks at low tide. When they beached the boat and went over to see, the body had disappeared. Anyhow there was no body and no funeral or nothing."

"Well, I hate to ruin your ghost story," said Reagan, "but the boy you are talking about was my dad. He fell into the surf, but his dog was able to pull him out. The dog is the one that died, not my dad. I am proof positive because here I am." Reagan added a smile to the end of that statement to let the group know that there were no hard feelings. The brunette smiled back, but the redhead's back was up, and she was not going to give.

"My grandma also says that your aunt, that potter lady, made a pact with the devil. No one has ever seen inside that old barn where she goes to do her work. Grandma says that the UPS guy said that he went to make a delivery one day. Your aunt didn't answer the door to the house, so he went to the old barn, thinking your aunt was out there. When he was walking to the barn, he heard this chanting, singing sound. He said it sounded like the hounds of hell were baying, and then he heard the devil's voice. He changed his mind and was turning to leave the package on the porch when all of a sudden, the barn door opened, and your aunt, her hair and eyes all wild, came out. He said he could see smoke and smelled fire and brimstone. He said that he could see the devil over your aunt's shoulder. He threw the package on the ground and never went back."

The redhead looked triumphant. The brunette looked ashamed, and the boy looked on, curious as to what was going to transpire. Reagan thought about that for a minute, slowly drawing another mouthful of malt. Man, that malt was really tasty. She was going to put some weight on this summer if she wasn't careful, she mused.

"So, this UPS guy heard the hounds of hell, heard the devil's voice, and saw the devil himself. It seems to me that the UPS guy is strangely familiar with the devil, don't you think?"

The brunette ducked her head to hide her smile, and the boy turned curiously toward the redhead, waiting for the fireworks. The redhead pouted and tossed her head.

"Well, I don't know about that. All I know is that I won't be caught dead going to Willow James' house, and you'd better watch your back. That place is haunted, mark my words."

"Well, I appreciate your concern, and I guess I won't count on you for movie night at my place."

With that Reagan flashed a final smile at the group and headed back to the lunch counter to finish her malt. The redhead gathered her purse and a package and looked expectantly at the young man who jumped to his feet and tossed some money on the table. They said their goodbyes to the brunette and left. The brunette put her own money on the table and made her way over to Reagan.

"Let's start this again, please. My name is Olivia, and I'm sorry about my goofy friends. Darcy doesn't mean any harm. She's just has a superiority complex." Olivia offered a smile to go along with the apology.

"You aren't responsible for your friend, but I appreciate the apology. Does she really believe that stuff?" asked Reagan, incredulously. "Do you?" she added as she watched Olivia's face.

"You have to understand, we've heard stories about that place all of our lives, and our parents heard stories all of their lives. Ghosts at the house on the cliff are an institution. You just believe it because, well... you just do. Then one day, when you hear someone telling the story to a newcomer, you realize just how silly it all sounds. But you have to understand, it is the town's tradition." Olivia blushed at the thought as she realized the whole explanation sounded really lame.

"You'll forgive me if I don't really buy into the whole thing, won't you?" asked Reagan. Olivia nodded. Reagan continued, "Does that mean you would come over for movie night?" The gauntlet was thrown, and Reagan waited to see if Olivia would pick it up.

"If somebody would have asked me that question yesterday, I would have said hell no, but yeah, I think I would. It doesn't mean I wouldn't be scared though. It's in my blood to be afraid of that place."

"Okay, I won't push it. So, what do you guys do around here for fun?" asked Reagan. "I'm enjoying reading my afternoons away, but I might need some companionship with people my own age one of these days."

"We spend a lot of time at Orchard Beach, but honestly, there's not a lot to do. Sometimes we head over to Portland, but not very often. For the most part, we just hang out." Olivia smiled apologetically. "We are kind of used to the quiet village life, and we like it. I have to go, so I'll see you around."

"Yeah, sure. See you around," offered Reagan, acutely aware that they hadn't exchanged phone numbers. Olivia started out the door of the store, stopped, and suddenly turned around.

"Reagan, I will take you up on that offer for a movie night some night. Just let me know when." She pulled out a scrap of paper from her purse and scribbled her phone number on it. Reagan tore it in half and did the same. Olivia left, and Reagan turned to finish her malt.

The waitress approached her with the check. "You know, you can't blame the kids for talking like they do."

Reagan looked up at the waitress who was peering down at her. Reagan hadn't noticed earlier that one of the waitress's eyes was clouded over, blind. The waitress went on.

"There've been stories about that place going way back. I heard 'em when I was a kid, and my kin 'fore that. Folks around here say some mighty unkind things about your aunt, not that I take any stock in it, mind you." The waitress was starting to wind up. "They say she made a pact with the devil. She locks herself in that barn, and no one is allowed to go in there when she's making her pots. And she's been wildly successful. People say the only reason is because she's no longer the one doing the pots. The devil is. A reporter came out to do a story about her for an art magazine an' she ran him off the property. She said she didn't want anyone taking no pictures of her studio or her while she was working. Things like that make people suspect. That an' people drowning and bodies disappearin' right off the beach. Mind my words, you be careful, now. You may not believe those stories, but they didn't come about out of thin air. There's a reason people talk. You just watch your back."

Reagan loudly slurped the last of her malt through the straw and smacked her lips.

"I appreciate your concern, but I'm fine. I don't believe all of that stuff. I don't mean to say that I don't respect your ideas, but I wasn't raised the same way you were. I will say that you make an excellent malt. So, thank you, and keep the change." With that, Reagan left the building.

CHAPTER 9

*T*wo days later, Reagan woke up to rain pounding on the windows. The wind was howling, and the house seemed to creak. She stretched and glanced over at her dresser. Her hairbrush lay sideways across the top, the same way she had found it for the last two mornings.

She tried to brush aside the voices of the kids at the Corner Grill telling her the house was haunted. There had to be a reasonable explanation, but try as she might, she couldn't figure out what happened every night. Before she went to bed, she would brush her hair, untangling her long tresses. She carefully lay the brush down in line with the perfume bottle and her hand lotion. Every morning, the brush was in the middle of the dresser and placed defiantly sideways.

She sighed. It probably should have creeped her out, but it was more perplexing. Surely there was a solid explanation, she just hadn't figured it out yet. She never was one for sleepwalking, but you were never too old to start. Swinging her legs over the side of the bed, she reached with her toes to find her slippers. They weren't there. What the hell? She always put her slippers next to the bed so that she could slip them right on. Despite the fact that it was summer, the hardwood floors were always chilly in the morning. Climbing out of bed, she got on the floor and looked under the bed... nothing. This is nuts. Turning around, she looked across the room. There, neatly placed in front of the rocking chair were her slippers. That didn't make sense. She hadn't sat in that rocking chair for days, preferring to read her books in bed, yet her slippers were sitting there as plain as day.

She walked over and reached down to grab them, and as she did, the rocking chair eased backward on its rockers and returned forward to its resting position. Now she was spooked. Even more frightening was the fact that the slippers, which had been parallel to each other, now sat crooked, the right one canted outward a little. A chill ran down her spine. Maybe the window was open a little, and the wind had blown the chair. This was an old house, and surely it was a draft. Not wanting to think about it anymore, Reagan grabbed her slippers and hustled downstairs still dressed in her pajamas, something she was not accustomed to doing.

Cora Rose was the only one in the kitchen. Willow had gone out of town to meet with a gallery owner down the coast. Cora flipped two pancakes on a plate and gestured to a pile of sausages on the table. It was obvious Cora Rose was not in a talkative mood today.

Reagan ate in silence, considering what her afternoon would entail. She was stabbing at a sausage link when her cell phone vibrated. Startled, she hadn't heard that sound in a while, she glanced down at the table where the phone sat announcing a text from Olivia. 'So, is that invitation still open for a movie day at your place, or am I being incredibly rude?'. Reagan smiled to herself. 'Sure,' she texted, 'if you have the nerves for it.'. The phone stayed blank. One minute. Two minutes. Shoot. Maybe she shouldn't have teased about that. Three minutes. 'Sorry, I had to let my dog out. I'm game. What time should I come over, and do you need anything? Popcorn, Chips?'

"Cora Rose, do we have any popcorn or snacks?" asked Reagan.

"There is some microwave popcorn in the little cupboard over the microwave. What, you don't like my pancakes?"

"No, Olivia is coming over today, and we were going to watch movies. I wanted to make some popcorn."

"Olivia Hodges? Caleb's girl?" Cora Rose was scowling fiercely.

"I guess. I met her at the Corner Grill. Why? What's the problem?"

Cora Rose looked down and angrily swiped the counter with her rag. "Caleb Hodges isn't going to like that one bit, and neither will Willow. Did you ask her if you can have guests, especially ones from the Hodges clan?"

"No, I didn't think I needed to. I live here now until my mom comes home, and I am going to have a social life. I don't intend to cause any problems, but I don't intend to be isolated. What's the beef between this Caleb person and my aunt?"

Cora Rose continued to wipe down the counter like she was trying to scrub away the surface.

"Cora?"

Cora spun around exasperated.

"Seriously, girl? Are you daft or something? You are telling me you don't know what goes on around here? Haven't you noticed things out of place, strange noises or voices? For the love of God, haven't you seen the eyes under the dining room table?" Cora Rose demanded.

Reagan wasn't ready to admit the singing she'd heard, the fact that her slippers had moved, or even the rocking chair rocking was remotely related to ghosts, or the supernatural, or any other gobbley-gook. All of that could be explained, but looking at Cora Rose, it was clear the woman really believed that there were freaking wolves under the damned table. The people of this town were unstable as hell. And what about Caleb?

"No, I don't think there are strange things going on here, and what does any of that have to do with Olivia's dad?

"Olivia's dad was driving on the road past the house one night. A woman ran out in front of his truck. He swerved to miss her but slammed the truck into the tree by the corner of the driveway. Willow heard the noise and went out with Wiley to find out what happened. Wiley went crazy with barking. Willow couldn't shut him up, and Caleb kept insisting that there was a woman. He was afraid he hit her with the corner of the truck. In fact, he pointed to what looked like blood on his front bumper. Willow told him he was crazy. By the time the sheriff came, Willow and Caleb had about come to blows. The sheriff investigated and found nothing. The blood on the bumper wasn't there when the sheriff checked it out. Caleb was cited with failure to control his vehicle. The sheriff left, and Caleb was left to wait with his truck until Randy Ovsberger came with his tow truck. Right before the tow came, Caleb watched the same woman walk across the road and head toward the house. He pointed her out to Willow, who was still standing there with Caleb. Wiley was looking at the woman and wagging his tail. Willow said that there was no one there. Then she looked at Caleb, smiled, and wished him a good night. She walked back to the house, but she didn't go alone. Caleb said he watched her walk next to the woman. It looked like Willow was having a conversation with her, and he swore the woman patted Wiley's head the entire way. He also said she was dressed like she came from another century, like she didn't belong here. He said they all walked into the house together. Trust me. He will not like that his daughter is coming over to hang out."

Reagan smiled sweetly and texted Olivia. 'We have popcorn here. When do you want to come over? Also, do you have a movie?'

"Okay, who invites a person over to watch a movie, but doesn't have a DVD player to watch the movie on?" Olivia stood in the parlor with Reagan, looking at the TV.

"I really didn't think about it. I only assumed. Who doesn't have a DVD player or something?"

"Apparently your aunt," said Olivia. "Is there another room with a TV?"

"You know, I'm not sure. Most of the time I've been in my room, the kitchen, or out on the porch if I'm not down on the rocks by the ocean," said Reagan.

Olivia looked at her sideways. "You mean the same rocks that your dad fell off of, but didn't die, but there was a body, and then there wasn't? Those rocks?"

Reagan smiled, remembering Darcy telling the story with relish and the deflated look she wore when Reagan explained the truth. "Yeah, those rocks. At least, I assume. I really don't know. No one has said anything about that here. In fact, no one has really said much about my family, this place, or anything. Willow and I eat breakfast every day in the big kitchen. Cora Rose makes it. Then Willow goes out to the barn to work, Cora Rose does stuff around the house until late morning, and I read or take walks. It's getting lonely."

"Don't you ever ask your aunt anything?"

"No. When she comes in from working, she usually grabs a sandwich or a snack and then goes to work in her office. Sometimes, we watch TV, but that's about it. I haven't really been here all that long, so there is still hope…"

"So, now what? I'm feeling brave, so can we explore this creepy old house? Darcy is going to flip when she finds out I was here."

Reagan stared at Olivia.

"Is that why you came? So, you can brag to your friends that you went to the crazy house?"

"Nope," said Olivia, completely without guilt, "I came because I wanted to watch a movie with you, but you have to admit, Darcy is going to flip."

"How about your dad? Is he going to flip, too?"

"Well, Dad doesn't need to know everything. How did you find out my dad wasn't fond of this place?"

"Cora Rose."

"Enough said," Olivia remarked. "So, can we explore?"

"Sure. I'll show you my room, first."

Reagan led Olivia up the stairs to the third floor. She showed her all the rooms that she had to choose from, and Olivia agreed that Reagan had picked the best one. When they left the room, Reagan headed for the narrow hall where her aunt's room was located, but Olivia started up the stairs to the next floor.

"Whoa," said Reagan, "we can't go up to the fourth floor."

"Why not?"

"I'm not sure, but my aunt says it is dangerous. I think the floor up there might be in disrepair or something. All I know is that I was told in no uncertain terms that it is off limits"

"Doesn't that make you want to go up there?" asked Olivia.

"It does, but I promised my mom I wouldn't disrespect my aunt's wishes. Come on, let's go through the old servant's quarters and down the back stairs." They stepped down the single step into the narrow hall and passed all the tiny rooms. When they reached the end of the hall they descended the steep, narrow stairs to the kitchen, then passed that floor and headed to the first floor. They opened an old wooden door and entered a stone room. The room was half underground with high, tall windows. It was dank and gloomy.

"Okay, this is creepy," said Olivia, as she brushed aside some cobwebs.

The ancient basement was filled with dusty tools and an old wooden cart. There were shelves along one wall that held murky remnants of canned fruit, perhaps peaches or apricots from years gone by. The light filtering in from the windows shone through the liquid, making the bulbous fruit look like entrails from a small animal.

The basement was broken up into rooms, each one holding groups of tools. One room had a large butcher block table, and the walls held rusty butcher knives. Evil looking hooks hung from the ceiling. Another room held hanks of reeds and several half-finished baskets. As they wandered from room to room, glimpsing into the past of a once prosperous farm, they meandered back into a dark corner. This was the opposite side of house, far away from the outside access door that could accommodate the wooden wagon they had first encountered.

They found themselves at the exterior wall of the basement. Cold, damp stones formed the foundation of the home that loomed above them. At the far end of the wall, in the darkest reaches of the basement, they came upon a heavy wooden door hung on thick wrought-iron hinges. A large iron handle held a padlock. In the upper reaches of the door, a window, covered in a heavy mesh of metal, leaked musty, rot-tainted air. Reagan's hairs stood up on the back of her neck. Olivia grabbed her hand. They stared at the door, a feeling of dread in the pits of their stomachs.

"What the hell is that door, and what's behind it?" whispered Olivia.

"I don't know, but it smells like decay. I don't much like it." They turned their backs to leave when a soft whisper, barely audible, shuddered through the air.

"Get. Out."

"Okay, did you hear that?" asked Olivia, her eyes wide.

"I don't know. I think it was the house creaking. This place is really old, you know? Let's go back upstairs." They turned and quickly made their way to the other side of the basement, to the welcoming door that led to the outside and the narrow stairs that would take them back to the kitchen. It was still raining, so they took the stairs up a floor and entered the kitchen.

"You didn't hear a voice down there, did you?" Olivia asked, clearly shaken.

"At first I thought I did, but I think it was just the sounds of the house. I mean, we were pretty amped up as it was, and our imaginations ran away with us. Maybe it was the wind blowing down through an opening in the basement or something, but I don't believe in ghosts or any other spooky crap like that. Do you? I mean, do you really?" asked Reagan as she opened the refrigerator and pulled out a couple of Pepsi's. She threw a bag of popcorn in the microwave.

"No, not really. Well, not like in the movies and stuff, but there are a lot of things that just can't be explained. Not only that, but why do we think we know everything? Why do we think that we are so superior that there is nothing beyond our comprehension that can't exist?"

"Well, you're a whole lot more open minded than I am."

Grabbing their Pepsi's and the popcorn, Reagan led the way out of the kitchen and headed toward the front of the house. Instead of walking into the parlor where the TV was located, she turned into a large, dark paneled room lined with bookshelves.

"This is crazy," said Olivia, whistling at the sight. "This house has its own library. How many books do you think are here?"

"I don't know. My first day here, I came into this room and got all excited because I figured I would have never ending reading material, but none of the books look interesting. They're old and dusty with boring covers."

"Yeah, none of them look all that great." They plopped down on the floor in the center of the room, munched on popcorn and looked over the contents of the shelves.

"Are those photo albums over there on that shelf?" Olivia pointed to a low shelf on the far side of the room.

"I don't know." Reagan got to her feet and made her way over. "It looks like there are a lot of old albums here."

She pulled a couple off the shelf. Olivia moved over, bringing the food with her. Leaning against the bookshelves, they opened the first album. Reagan flipped through a few pages and was stunned when she saw her father's face staring at her from the page. He was young, but his gray eyes and boyish smile were unmistakable.

"What's wrong?" asked Olivia.

"That's my dad," Reagan whispered. They both studied the picture, and Olivia murmured her uncomfortable condolences.

As they turned the pages, they caught a glimpse of Wolf and Willow's life, captured in film. Fishing on a pier, a class picnic, a ski trip, all with Wolf's patented smile shining from the page. Willow looked carefree, a normal kid in a time gone by. Then Reagan turned the page and saw an eight by ten senior picture of her father. His smile had changed, and his eyes looked haunted. The boyish, carefree countenance was replaced by a gaunt young man who carried a world of pain on his shoulders.

"He looks so sad," Olivia said.

"He really does." That was the last picture of Reagan's dad. There were a few more of Willow and presumably their parents, Reagan's grandparents, but Wolf had completely disappeared from the record.

Olivia's phone chirped, and she stood up, gathering her empty Pepsi can. "Mom says she needs me to stop by the store and pick up some things for dinner, so I need to head home."

"So, are you going to tell your friends you survived a day at the crazy lady's house?"

"Nah, it's none of their business. You can tell them when we go to the movies in Portland Friday night. If you want to go, that is."

"Sure, as long as Darcy doesn't mind."

"Forget Darcy. She's not a bad person, just a bit dramatic. You'll get used to it."

CHAPTER 10

*A*fter Olivia left, Reagan gathered the Pepsi cans and empty popcorn bag and tossed them in the kitchen garbage. It was still gloomy outside, so she decided to explore more of the albums. Heading back toward the library with Wiley padding silently beside her, she suddenly heard the faintest sound of singing. Wiley stopped and cocked his head, his ears lifting. Reagan strained her ears. Was she really hearing singing? She was aware of the rain pelting the side of the house and the sighing of the wind, but still, the faint strains of singing were coming from the library.

Wiley's tail began a slow wag, and he moved ahead of Reagan pushing himself through the library door. Still wagging, he walked over and leaned against an old velvet covered settee and stared upward, raptly. His ears pressed down against his head, and he stretched his neck to the side. If Reagan didn't know better, she would swear Wiley was getting his neck scratched. Crazy dog, she thought. Then she stopped in her tracks.

Sitting on the settee was one of the photo albums. This one looked old, with a leather embossed cover. She didn't remember putting an album there. She glanced over at the stack that she and

Olivia pulled off the shelf. They were still piled neatly on the floor where they had been sitting. No, no one had put an album on the piece of furniture.

Reagan heard a light musical laugh, and Wiley got up lazily and moved over to Reagan, softly licking her hand as if to say everything was going to be okay. She absently reached down, scratching the dog's soft ears. This day was just getting creepier.

Convincing herself that Olivia had dropped the album there on her way out, Reagan walked over to pick it up. Settling on the stiff velvet couch, she opened the album and was transported into a time long ago. Ancient brown and white photos were held in the album under ornate paper frames. Spidery old-fashioned script graced the pages, naming the stiffly posed people in the formal poses. Reagan idly flipped her way through the album, being careful not to cause harm to the decaying pages. The ancient clothing looked constricting and uncomfortable, yet the dresses were dripping with delicate lace making them exquisite.

She paused at one page, struck with the beauty of the young lady in the portrait. Long ringlet curls cascaded down the delicate shoulders of the stunning girl. Unlike the other grim ladies in the album, all prim and proper, this girl's eyes were lit up, and she was smiling with delight. Everything about her was happy and full of life. Delicate lace covered the bodice of her summery white dress, and in her gloved hand, she held an ornate metal starfish. Deciphering the faded antique writing below the picture, Reagan read, *Adelaide.*

She stared at the picture of the girl who had lived in her room, the girl that Cora Rose said was dragged down the stairs. Reagan could easily imagine this girl in the beautiful blue bedroom. Both the room and the girl exuded happiness and light. "Adelaide," Reagan whispered. A tinkle of laughter reached her ears, and Wiley wagged his tail again. Reagan snapped the album shut. I'm losing it, she thought. Now I am imaging ghosts laughing. Enough of this crap. She put the albums away. Retrieving her book from her room, she went out on the front porch to watch the rain and read the evening away.

It was late in the evening when Willow's car drove up the driveway. Wiley raised his head from the porch floor and his tail slapped a rhythmic thud, thud as he waited patiently to greet his master. Reagan stirred stiffly as she put down the most recent crime novel she was reading.

"Hello, Aunt Willow. You look tired."

"Yep, it was a long day." Willow sighed as she lowered herself into a rocking chair.

"Would you like me to get you a Pepsi and a sandwich?" asked Reagan. Willow looked up surprised.

"You don't have to do that."

"I know I don't, but I would like to."

"Yes, that would be nice. You know I like tomatoes on my sandwich, right?" Willow asked.

"I know just how you like it. I'll be right out." Reagan skipped into the house, eager to be of some help. She quickly made two sub sandwiches, complete with thinly sliced tomato and mayo on Willow's. Grabbing the two plates and shoving the Pepsi under her arm, she headed back out to the porch. Willow startled when the screen door slammed.

"Oh, I'm sorry. I didn't mean to wake you," stammered Reagan.

"Just resting my eyes," said Willow as she reached for the Pepsi and the offered plate. "That looks amazing, thanks." They settled themselves comfortably next to each other and ate silently while listening to the creak of the rockers on the old wooden porch. It would be dusk soon, and the frogs were beginning to sing in the pond by the barn.

Willow sighed when she finished. "That really hit the spot. Thanks."

"Did your visit with the galleries go well?"

"Actually, they did. I have a huge order to complete. It will keep me busy most of the summer. I have to deliver it by August first, which means I will be practically living in the barn, but it will pay the bills."

"Willow, do you like being a potter? I mean, would you rather go to an office and know you are getting a paycheck every week?"

"Not in a million years. This is hard work, and it's feast or famine. There are long stretches where I won't get any work, and then it all hits at once, but there is nothing I would rather be doing. I have simple needs except for keeping up this house, so I am glad I can make a living this way."

"This house is important to you, isn't it?"

"Yes, it is. I would do anything to keep this house. It's been in our family since it was built. Your entire family was born here, except for you."

"Seriously? You and my dad were actually born in this house?"

"Yes, we were, and our daddy before that, and his daddy before that, and his daddy... get the idea?"

"Was Adelaide born here?"

"Of course, she was. She was a James. What do you know of Adelaide?"

"Not much. Only that you said she wouldn't mind if I had her room, and that Cora Rose said she was dragged down the basement stairs. That's a story I want to hear. I had forgotten all about that stuff until I saw her picture in an old album in the library."

"So, you spent this rainy day exploring the albums, huh?"

"Yep. I saw pictures of you and my dad when you guys were in high school. There were some great pictures, but then they stopped after his senior picture. Then I found the old album and saw Adelaide's picture. She was beautiful. So, who was she?"

"Adelaide is your great-great-great aunt. She's a kind soul, but her heart was broken young."

"You talk about her as if she is still alive."

"Well, isn't she? She is still alive in you and me. We are James', and we are linked. Her essence is still in that room. It looks the same as when she lived in it. Her spirit is all through this house."

"She seemed like she was a happy girl. Did she sing?"

"So, you fancy you have heard her singing?"

"No, I'm certain it was just the wind I heard. I don't know why I asked that question. Did she get married? Did she have children? Where are her ancestors, and do they ever come here to the house?"

Willow sat quietly, gathering her thoughts. She spoke carefully and softly when she finally answered. "Adelaide died very young. On the morning of her wedding day, she fell from the cliff top to the rocks below. It was a terrible tragedy," said Willow. Reagan sat stunned. It was straight from some ridiculous romance novel. She figured Willow was pulling her leg.

"Right," said Reagan, "and she haunts the cliffs on a full moon."

"Of course not! She haunts the house on a daily basis. Thanks for the sandwich, I'll see you in the morning. Remember, do not stay out here after dark, and be certain to lock the door." With that Willow went into the house and left Reagan sitting in the rocking chair with her mouth wide open.

Reagan regained her composure and looked down at the Lab, who looked back at her with his liquid brown eyes. "Wiley, all of these people here in this town are crazy. My aunt is crazy, Cora Rose is crazy, Olivia might be a little crazy, and we know her father is. Please tell me you aren't crazy, too?" Wiley thumped his tail, then got up and walked to an empty rocking chair. He raised his paw, as if to say hello, then flattened his ears on the side of his head and smiled his happy Lab smile. Reagan could have sworn he was getting the top of his head petted, but there was no one there.

"Come on you stupid dog. Let's go inside." She picked up her book and her empty Pepsi can and held the screen door for the dog. He reluctantly got up, licked the air, and then followed Reagan into the house. She locked the door and threw away the garbage, turning out the lights as she started toward her bedroom.

As she passed through the dark dining room, she heard Wiley give a low, throaty growl. It was so menacing, she stopped in her tracks. "What's wrong boy?" She looked down at Wiley to see him staring across the dining room at the huge antique table. His growl deepened and grew louder. Reagan's heart beat harder in her chest. As she peered into the gloom of the darkened dining room, her eyes tried to adjust. What was wrong with Wiley?

She took a step toward the table. Wiley leapt at her, throwing his body in front of her, and leaned hard against her knees. His hackles raised all along his back. His lips curled completely over the top of his nose, and his long canine teeth were bared. "Wiley, what is it?"

There was a note of hysteria in her voice that she didn't recognize. Suddenly, in the dark underneath the table, she saw strange red reflections, like eyes in the dark. Wiley let out a sharp bark. The office door snapped open, and Willow stood in the door frame. "Wiley, out!" commanded Willow. The light from the office dispersed the shadows in the dining room and the only thing under the table were the legs of the numerous chairs surrounding it.

"Reagan, is there something wrong?"

"I...I don't know," Reagan stammered. "Wiley just went a little crazy. He just started growling and wouldn't let me near the table. I don't know what is going on, but I thought..."

"You thought what, dear?"

"Nothing. It's silly. I just saw a strange reflection or something. What was up with Wiley, though?"

"Probably saw a mouse or something. I'll tell Cora Rose to set out some traps tomorrow. She'll like that." Willow grinned at the thought and wished a shaken Reagan goodnight.

Reagan nodded mutely and started up the stairs. She was still a little frightened. It was like she had seen eyes under the table. Cora Rose's wolves? No, she was not that stupid to think that there were wolves under a dining room table.

CHAPTER 11

*R*eagan woke up to sunshine streaming in her windows. Despite the upsetting evening she'd had the night before, she had slept like a rock.

Wiley put his two front paws on her bed and washed her face with his big sloppy tongue in a good morning greeting. Out of habit, she glanced over at her dresser, expecting to see her hairbrush there where it was every morning since she had moved in. She was shocked it wasn't on the dresser. She moved her gaze over to the vanity where she had lined up her brush, lotion, and perfume the night before. There it lay, in perfect position, just as she had left it. She smiled to herself. This was the first night she felt she had slept soundly, and her brush was where it belonged. Willow must have been right. She must have been sleepwalking because she was in a strange place. Well, strange is certainly true Reagan thought, but at least her hairbrush mystery was solved.

After a quick shower, she skipped down the stairs. The smell of maple syrup, coffee, and waffles was calling to her. She smiled to herself, feeling spoiled. How was she going to go back to not eating breakfast once she was home and school started? She was really going to miss Cora Rose's cooking.

"Good morning, Cora Rose. The wonderful aroma of your food roused me this morning, and I can't wait to eat those waffles."

"You're in an annoyingly good mood for some who saw the wolves last night," Cora Rose muttered. "Now your aunt wants me to set out stupid traps to catch non-existent mice, because no one wants to admit that this place is possessed by demons. If Willow thinks I am going to crawl under that table to put a trap, she has another thing coming. I will not go there." Cora Rose punctuated her statement by waving her spatula wildly about. Bits of waffle flew off and Wiley snapped the air in an attempt to capture the minuscule crumbs.

"Cora Rose, if it upsets you that much, I'll put the traps under the table. There aren't any wolves, and I don't believe in letting fear get the best of me. Just tell me what to do, and I'll do it," said Reagan as she helped herself to a golden waffle and poured a generous amount of pure maple syrup on top. Sliding three sausage links into the pools of syrup that flooded the sides of her plate, she walked her way back to the kitchen table humming to herself.

"What are you humming, and where did you hear that?" gasped Cora Rose.

"Hmmm?" asked Reagan absently, as she checked her cell-phone for texts from her mom.

"That song you were humming? Where did you hear it?"

"I have no idea. I really didn't realize I was humming. What has you so upset on this gorgeous morning?" Reagan pushed.

"You do. You and your arrogant, youthful, citified ways," scolded Cora Rose. "You come here and act like you don't see what's going on. You act like you're too good for the likes of those of us who have lived here all our lives and know what goes on here. Well, mark my words, you will pay for your arrogance. Just you watch."

With that Cora Rose swept out of the kitchen, carrying a

handful of mouse traps. Reagan watched, speechless, as Cora Rose passed the dining room table and placed a few traps near the sideboard and then continued on into the front entrance hall. Bat-shit crazy, thought Reagan. Certifiably, bat-shit crazy. Still, Cora Rose's threats were beginning to bother her. No one liked being told that they were going to pay. It made Reagan nervous. Shaking it off, she finished her breakfast and then grabbed the two remaining baited mousetraps from the counter near the garbage. She waltzed into the dining room, got down on her hands and knees and stared under the massive, antique dining room table.

Shimmying on her stomach, Reagan inched her way under the table, scooting to the far end at the back of the dim dining room. The table was long, ten chairs lining each side. When she reached the end, she placed a trap under the chair at the foot of the table. Turning, she started to inch her way back, figuring on placing the last trap at the halfway point.

What the hell? She felt a hot, moist breath on her ankle. Looking back at her feet, she didn't see anything, but there it was again, the hot breath bearing down on her. She started to crawl faster and kicked out with her feet. She connected with a chair, sending it scooting backward. She heard a snarl and felt a searing pain in her left ankle. Yelping with a final effort, she scrambled out from under the table. She looked down to see blood streaming from a gash in her leg.

"I told you so." Cora Rose stood in front of her with a menacing smirk. Reagan stared at her and then looked back at the dark space between the chairs. Nothing. "Come on, let's clean you up."

As they headed toward the kitchen, they were startled by a loud SNAP. Turning, they saw the tiny body of a mouse caught in the jaws of one of the traps under the table. Reagan looked at Cora Rose triumphantly, who merely scowled at her and pointed at Reagan's ankle.

In the kitchen, Reagan examined the jagged gash in her skin. She couldn't for the life of her figure out what had caused it. She could explain her imagination running away from her thinking she could feel the panting breath of an imaginary wolf, but the cut in her skin was far from imaginary. Willow walked in as Cora Rose poured hydrogen peroxide on the wound.

"What happened?" asked Willow.

"Wolf bite," replied Cora Rose

"Right," said Willow. "Reagan have you had your rabies vaccination?"

"What the hell?" said Reagan

"I'm kidding. Have you had a tetanus shot within the last seven years?"

"Yeah, I had to get one before I went to camp two years ago."

"Good, then there is nothing to worry about."

"Ya wanna explain to her just what bit her?" asked Cora Rose

"Where did it happen?" asked Willow.

"I told you, it's a wolf bite. It happened under the dining room table. Reagan decided to put mousetraps under the table, and a wolf got her," said Cora Rose with a creepy satisfaction.

"And I caught a mouse, too," said Reagan, smirking at Cora Rose. "It's still in the trap. Cora Rose refuses to get it. As soon as she is done torturing my leg, I can go get it," Reagan said with bravado.

"No need. I'll go fetch it myself." With that Willow stalked off to the dining room.

"Well, Cora Rose, aren't you worried about Willow getting attacked by the wolves?"

"They won't bother Willow. They know better. Willow has a pact..."

"CORA ROSE," Willow reprimanded, "here is the mouse. Please dispose of it, and Reagan, here is the wolf tooth that bit your leg." Willow produced a large splinter, the pointy end stained with fresh blood.

"Satisfied?" asked Reagan, looking pointedly at Cora Rose.

"No, I would expect Willow would have a perfectly good explanation. Don't matter. I'm telling you, you was bit by a wolf. Now stay clear of the dining room table, or they will grab you and drag you down to the cellar."

"Cora Rose, don't you have linens to change? Reagan, if you're okay, I am going out to the studio to work. Don't expect to see me today. I have to start on my large order. If you need me for anything, just ring the large bell by the barn door, and I will come out. Okay?" Reagan nodded in agreement, acutely aware of the glowering look Cora Rose was giving her. Reagan couldn't wait to escape to the ocean and away from this craziness!

CHAPTER 12

*W*ith a fresh bandage on her leg, Reagan slipped out the screen door and onto the porch. The day was crisp, and the dazzling blue sky was fresh and clear. Yesterday's bad weather had washed clean the world.

Wiley bounded up beside Reagan, eager to join her on an adventure. They walked past the barn where Reagan could her the radio blasting 60s music. She chuckled to herself thinking of Darcy's story of the UPS man hearing chanting. In this back-woods town, the UPS man probably would mistake rap music for chanting with the devil. Smiling at her own wit, Reagan made her way to the cliff and the trail that led to the ocean.

The waves were crashing this morning, which shocked her. The day was so calm and beautiful. She expected the ocean to be the same way. She had been warned enough about how dangerous the rocks were when the ocean was rough, so she was extra careful to stay up against the cliff and away from the reach of the waves. The tide was out, so she had lots of room to walk. In a few hours, when the tide started to come in, she would have to be careful. As rough as the ocean was today, there wouldn't be any room between the battering waves and the cliff face once the tide was all the way in. Still, there was plenty of time to sit on the rocks and enjoy the day.

She had brought her book down and a beach towel she had found. She folded the towel to make a comfortable seat and leaned back against the cliff. Gulls whirled overhead, crying in the wind. They would dive into the rough chop and surface, sometimes with a fish in their beaks. Then they would bob on the waves, not caring that the ocean was a rough riot of swirling, crashing water. Reagan envied them that they could float, unconcerned about their safety. She opened her book and became lost in the intricacies of her current serial killer character.

Engrossed, she never saw or heard Seth approach. He stood, watching her as she read, close enough to touch her. He waited. Within a few minutes, Reagan had this uncanny feeling that she wasn't alone. Looking up she gasped to see Seth just a foot away.

"When did you get here? How long have you been watching me?" Seth just shrugged, a slight grin playing around his lips. "Well, it's not very nice to do that. I don't like people sneaking up on me!"

"What did you do to your leg?" asked Seth, calmly.

"A wolf bit me," Reagan answered flippantly. Seth paled slightly. "I'm kidding, sheesh," said Reagan. "Seriously, is everyone around here crazy?"

"What makes you think that everyone is crazy?"

"Well, Cora Rose thinks, oh never mind, or I'll start sounding crazy, too."

"Mind if I sit with you?"

"Not at all. Hang on, let me unfold this towel so we can share it. It's softer for your butt that way."

"My butt can handle the rocks, but thanks." The both got situated and stared silently out to sea. Seth sat close to Reagan, and she became acutely aware of his slightly citrus and spicy scent. He smelled clean and fresh.

"What?" asked Seth

"Nothing," said Reagan, her face coloring slightly. "I was thinking how I loved the way the ocean smelled."

"Uh huh," said Seth, as he slid his eyes to her. Her stomach fluttered a little. His eyes had taken on a green hue today, reflecting the color of the turbulent ocean.

"So, ah, what do you do with your day?" asked Reagan. "Do you have a job or anything?"

"I work with my father. We fish."

"So, it's too rough to fish today?"

"Nope."

"Then why aren't you fishing?"

"We already did. The boat has been out, and we brought back nets full of fish. They have already been taken to market."

"It's still morning. How did you do that?"

"We were out very early, and it was a good day."

"So, you never did tell me. Where do you live?"

"Over there," Seth gestured down the coast. "I live beyond the curve of the cliff."

"I live up in the house above the cliff."

"I know," said Seth.

"How do you know that?"

"Because you don't live down near me, and this trail leads up the cliff to the old house. So, obviously you live there."

"Have you always lived here in Littleport?"

"All my life," said Seth

"So, you know all the stories about the house I live in?"

"I know a lot about the house you live in, but I'm not sure of the stories you are talking about. If you mean the things the people around here gossip about, I don't pay much attention to that. People like to think all kinds of things. It gives them something to talk about."

"That's exactly what I think. These people love drama, so they embellish every story with fiction and lose the fact. Take this morning. If Cora Rose has her way, by tonight the entire town will think I was bitten by wolves under the dining room table. If I am not careful, she will have them believe I was drug down the basement stairs by a pack of dining room wolves like old Adelaide. People are nuts. Don't you think? Seth?" Reagan glanced over at Seth to find him staring off at the ocean with a wistful look on his face. "What, don't tell me you believe that stuff?"

"Adelaide was drug down the basement stairs, but I don't think it was wolves that did it." Seth's jaw clenched, the muscle working in and out along his cheek.

"Wait, you know the story of Adelaide? She was alive, like eons ago. Why do you know the story?"

"Most people have heard it."

"Wait, what do you think drug her down the basement stairs," asked Reagan.

"The embodiment of pure evil. That's what I think."

"I knew it. You're crazy, too. What was it, the bogey man? An evil poltergeist? What?"

"No, I don't think it was the bogey man. Don't you think there are people in the world that are just plain bad, pure evil?" Seth glanced at the cover of her book. On it was a picture depicting a woman who had been murdered, blood splattered everywhere. A knife was prominently displayed above her body.

"I guess you're right. People can be evil, but where does everyone get this wolf story?" Reagan asked. Seth shrugged his shoulders but didn't meet Reagan's eyes. She couldn't decide if he believed in that crap or not. He was being evasive. Despite that, the man was definitely easy on the eyes. That's for damn sure.

They sat companionably for the next hour. Seth told her about the kinds of fish they preferred to catch from the sea and explained how a lobster pot worked. They became comfortable with each other, and the sun made them lazy and warm. Reagan closed her eyes, soaking in the soft rays of late morning.

"How do you feel about spiders?" Seth asked.

"I hate them, why?" Reagan stiffened.

"Don't freak, but you have one on your shoulder." Seth reached over and knocked the spider off of her. The minute he brushed her shoulder with his fingertips, a jolt of electricity vibrated through her body, and an unholy scream echoed off the cliffs.

"What the hell?" exclaimed Reagan. She peered up the cliff, searching for the offending sound. She could just see the fourth floor of the house peeking over the top of the cliff.

"Just a gull screaming. I think one got in a squabble with another over the ownership of a fish." Reagan nodded, accepting the explanation, but then she saw what looked like a face peering out of one of the windows on the fourth floor. Reagan squinted and looked again, but all she could see was the reflection of the sun in the upper floor windows, and then another gull let out a bloodcurdling scream. Reagan jumped knocking into Seth.

"Hey, are you okay?" Seth took hold of Reagan's shoulders, looking at her face anxiously.

"Um, yeah," said Reagan, embarrassed, "I just hate the screaming of the gulls."

"You'll get used to it," said Seth. He still held her shoulders, and his eyes locked into hers. A tingle of electricity seemed to pulse from his hands and travel to her stomach where the butterflies wreaked havoc again. He reached up and gently brushed aside a strand of hair from her face. "You're fine. The gulls won't hurt you."

"I know, but it sounds more like a woman screaming, and I swear I just saw a face in the fourth-floor window." Reagan's face colored as she realized just how stupid she sounded. Despite that, she glanced over her shoulder again up at the old house. Seth gave her shoulders a little squeeze before he let go. She found herself immensely disappointed. Maybe this is why all the women in romance novels are simpering weak women. Men hold their shoulders when they think the damsel is afraid. Well, she was not one of those silly females. Yes, the holding was certainly nice, but she could hold her own!

Seth looked at her with amusement dancing in his eyes. "What are you thinking?"

"Nothing."

"Right, nothing. You just got the look of a bulldog guarding his territory. I'm sorry I touched you. I'm sorry if it bothered you." He smiled, waiting.

"Oh, no, it was fine, I liked it." Oh crap. What did she just say? "I mean, oh my God, I should say thanks, or... shit, I've got to go." With her face turning a bright shade of scarlet, Reagan grabbed her towel and book and headed up the trail, not even taking a minute to look back.

"Okay, then. Bye," said Seth. "Will I see you tomorrow?"

"Maybe," yelled Reagan, as she raised her hand in a casual wave, trying to walk calmly away despite the fact that she was mortified.

The next day, Reagan once again headed down to the beach. This time she had her backpack with her. She had a larger blanket to sit on, her book, and a couple of bottles of water. She was going to spend the day there reading, but if Seth showed up, well, there was enough blanket to share and a bottle of water for him if he wanted it.

The ocean was calmer today, and the gentle crash of the waves lulled Reagan into an impromptu nap in the sun. Wiley curled up next to her with his big, square bony head resting in her lap. As she dozed, Reagan dreamed of a dark hallway with lots of doors. Someone was calling to her, but she couldn't tell which door the person was behind. At first it sounded like her mom, but it wasn't. The voice became increasingly insistent that Reagan find her and help her, and Reagan became more frantic that she wouldn't be able to find this person and help them in time. She methodically tried every door, but as she worked her way down the hall, she discovered that they were all locked. The voice screamed for help, and Reagan became wild with fear. Then one long, agonizing scream pierced the air.

Reagan startled awake as Seth gently nudged her shoulder. She looked around wildly. Her dream was so vivid. Where was she? What had happened, and who was screaming? As she became more and more awake, she realized that Seth was there trying to wake her up, and the gulls were wheeling overhead again, screaming their blood-curdling cry.

"Reagan, what's wrong? You're shaking." Seth crouched down and gathered her into his arms. Reagan leaned into his shoulder breathing in his citrus scent.

"I had a terrible dream. Someone needed my help. I was in a long corridor with rooms on both sides. I could hear the person calling for help, but I couldn't find which door, and they were locked. Then there was this terrible screaming." Reagan shuddered against Seth, grateful for the strong arms locked around her. His hand stroked her silky hair as he held her, rocking her slightly.

"It was just a dream and noisy gulls. Your mind just turned the cry of the gulls into a dream that's all. You're safe now."

He lifted her chin, forcing her to look into his eyes. Today, they were gray like the ocean during the rain. She gazed into them, lost in their depth. Calm filled her soul and her trembling stopped. Still, he held her, cupping her cheek, his thumb gently brushing across her lower lip. Her breath hitched, and the stomach butterflies returned with a vengeance. He leaned close and softly brushed his lips against hers. They were cold, as if he had been in the ocean swimming, yet they kindled a fire deep in her belly. She stared up at him, willing him to give her more. He groaned and threaded her hair through his fingers at the back of her head. He crushed her toward him and kissed her hungrily. She gave back, her hot lips bruising his, warming the cold that was his, while the surrounding air reverberated with heart-breaking screams.

Abruptly, Seth pulled away. The air was filled with electricity, and the seagulls were diving around them. Seth batted at one large gull as it swooped at Reagan's head. Wiley leapt to his feet, jumping in the air, snapping at the annoying birds.

"Why are they so close to us?" asked Reagan. "What are they doing, and why are they acting weird?"

"I don't know, but they are really getting aggressive," answered Seth, as he threw a rock at another swooping bird. Seth moved away from Reagan and settled himself on the folded blanket. The flock of gulls wheeled around and headed out to sea.

"That was really weird," said Reagan, "I didn't know gulls attacked people."

"Well, they really didn't hurt us. They just came close. Are you all right now?"

"If I said, no, would you kiss me again?" said Reagan boldly.

"Maybe, let's try it and see."

"Then no, I am not all right now," whispered Reagan.

The corners of Seth's mouth twisted up slightly, and he leaned toward her, taking her hands in his and kissed her gently on the mouth. Again, his lips were chilled, his hands cool over hers. He deepened the kiss, drawing her nearer. She closed her eyes and sighed and then screamed. A gull's talons tore into her hair, scratching her scalp, ripping at her and beating her head with its wings. Seth jumped up and grabbed the gull, slamming it into the rocks. Reagan sobbed and watched as Seth killed the bird in front of her, twisting its neck as a final assurance that it was dead. He wiped his hands on his pants and drew her close, parting her hair to check the wound.

"That bird scratched your head. You probably need to get something on it. You are having a run of bad luck, aren't you?

Didn't you say a wolf bit you yesterday?" Seth teased. Reagan stared at him, surprised at the teasing note in his voice. She had just been attacked by a bird, and he was making a joke.

"I don't think this is funny," she said hotly, angrily swiping her sleeve across her face to erase the remnants of her tears.

"Neither do I," murmured Seth, "and I am going to make certain this shit stops." He brushed away the last tear on her cheek and gave her a quick hug. "You need to take care of that cut, and I need to go. Will I see you tomorrow?"

"I don't know. I am not interested in another bird attack."

"Don't worry. It won't happen again," promised Seth, the muscles his jaws flexing as he clenched his teeth. "I'll make sure to protect you next time. Are you okay to go back to the house?"

"Yeah," said Reagan reluctantly. "I'll be fine." With that, she gathered her belongings and started up the trail. She turned to tell Seth that she wasn't mad at him, but he was already gone, nowhere to be seen.

CHAPTER 13

 rustrated and angry, Reagan made her way back up the trail. She felt abandoned by Seth, and she couldn't believe she was attacked by seagulls. Wiley padded next to her, his head down, sulking. He looked at her with his big, brown, liquid eyes, as if apologizing for not protecting her. She reached down and absently patted his sun-warmed head.

She thought about Seth's lips on hers, cold and salty. Her stomach quivered at the memory. Strange, she thought, how chilly Seth felt despite the sun pounding down on them. She hugged herself. He may have been chilly, but he sure lit a fire in her. His kiss was delicious, and she hoped it would happen again. She could use a little excitement of the normal teenage variety as opposed to the wacky things these people seemed to always talk about.

Humming to herself, and feeling happy despite her wounds, she let herself into the house. In the kitchen cupboard she found a first aid kit, and she smeared antibiotic cream into the scratch on her head. It was tender, and it made her angry all over again. Luckily, Cora Rose seemed to be gone, so she didn't have to deal with the woman's speculation as to why the gulls acted crazy.

Cora Rose would probably blame it on wolves or ghosts, or something insane like that.

Reagan put away the first aid kit and snapped off the kitchen light. Walking through the dining room, she saluted the table with a defiant middle finger and went into the library. She carefully pulled the ancient album off the shelf and opened to the page with Adelaide's portrait. This is where she had closed the album, but now she wanted to see the rest of the pictures. Curious, she studied the visage of her long ago aunt. Could she see a family resemblance?

Picking up the album, she left the library and headed upstairs to her room. Sitting at the dressing table in front of the mirror, she held up the album, switching her gaze from her own reflection to the picture of Adelaide and back again. Was it her imagination, or did they look a lot alike? The jawline was the same, the same heart-shaped face. They both had high, delicate cheekbones, but Adelaide's nose was more refined and slightly turned up. They shared well defined eyebrows, although Adelaide's eyes looked like they might have been light-colored, perhaps a blue, but in the sepia-toned photo, it was hard to tell. The two could definitely pass as sisters that was certain.

Reagan carried the album to the rocking chair. Settling in, she turned the page carefully. The next portrait showed a young woman who stared defiantly at the camera with an almost scowling attitude. Her eyes were dark, and her hair was a wild array of long, inky tresses. Her dress was devoid of the dripping lace that adorned Adelaide's bodice. Underneath the portrait was the name Ariana. Reagan studied Ariana's eyes. They felt menacing and unkind. She was a sharp contrast to Adelaide.

The other album held more portraits of stiff looking people in formal poses. Reagan idly paged through, losing interest. These pictures captured the style of dress and hair of the time period, but there were no pictures that depicted a slice of the peoples' everyday lives. Reagan considered the thousands of pictures she'd snapped with no thought. She took pictures of food and her toes on the beach, selfies of her crazy faces and her friends just hanging out. Someone could easily see what kind of person she was just by the photos she had taken and those taken of her. These ancient portraits only showed the formal side of these peoples' world. They didn't open the door to their hopes and joys, or hard work to survive. As Reagan absently turned the last page she gasped. There were two pictures of babies. One beautiful child, dressed in a long, snowy white christening gown, lay in an ornate wicker bassinet, her chubby cheeks and eyes crinkled in an unintentional baby smile. The other portrait was of a baby also in a snowy white gown, only her face was still, her eyes closed as she lay dead in a satin-lined casket.

What the hell? They took pictures of dead babies? Who does that? Reagan closed the book in disgust. She couldn't wrap her head around the idea of taking a baby portrait of a dead child. Was it the same child as in the picture next to it, or was it another? She was curious, but really didn't want to ask Willow or Cora Rose, especially Cora Rose. She would say the baby had been attacked by wolves under the dining room table!

Reagan took the album back to the library and stopped in the kitchen to get a glass of milk. She decided to finish out the day reading her last library book so she could take a trip into town the next day to return her books and take out new ones.

Trotting upstairs to her room, she retrieved her book off her nightstand. As she was walking out the door, she noticed a small book laying on the rocking chair. Where the heck had that come from? Setting down the glass of milk and her library book, she crossed to the rocking chair and stared at the book. It was old leather with an ornate, heavily embossed cover. The word 'journal' graced the cover in fine, gold script letters. Reagan continued to stare, waiting for the book to disappear. After all, it just appeared there. She was just in this room, and this book hadn't been on the rocking chair. Cora Rose was gone, and Willow was in the barn working. Books didn't just appear out of thin air. Someone was screwing with her, and she didn't think it was funny.

She snatched the journal off the chair and immediately felt guilty because crumbs of disintegrated leather from the cover floated to the floor. She loosened her grip and carried the journal carefully. Leaving her book, she picked up her milk and headed out to the porch. First, she was going to take a look at the journal. Then, she was going to sort this out. She was determined to find out just who put that book on the chair even if it meant disturbing Willow in the barn when she was working.

Wiley wandered up to Reagan as she lowered herself to the porch swing. He sniffed the journal in her hand and wagged his tail happily. His nose worked harder at sniffing, and his tail followed suit, wagging until his whole butt was wiggling. Reagan laughed at his antics and sipped on her milk. What was with this silly dog? She carefully opened the journal and looked at the first page. The name Adelaide was written in a graceful hand in a faded blue ink. Under the name were doodles of flowers and leaves, and even an attempt at a stylized bird.

Reagan felt a little thrill course through her. This was Adelaide's journal, written in her hand so, so many years ago. She thought back to when she was looking at the pictures, disappointed that they didn't really show a glimpse into the people's lives. Now she was holding a journal that well may give her personal details into the world of the girl who used to sleep in the very bed Reagan slept in every night.

~ *Adelaide's Journal*

My name is Adelaide James. Papa came home from Boston today and brought me this beautiful journal. He told me that everyone has a story to tell, but not everyone gets to read it. This is for my most private thoughts I can't share with anyone. Papa winked when he gave it to me. He knows I am growing up, but I wonder if he knows how I feel about S. I hope not. I'm not yet ready to share that with anyone, and I don't want Papa to disapprove. I am afraid he will. He would say S. is of a lower station in life and that I am destined for a more genteel gentleman. Hogwash. S. is as gentle and kind as any gentleman. He is not coarse or crude. I do care for him greatly, but I am afraid of my feelings. He stirs in me something I don't understand, but I love the feeling of butterflies in my stomach.

Reagan smiled at the mention of butterflies, recalling the fluttering feeling she knew all too well. Captivated with Adelaide's story, she tucked her feet under her and settled deeper into the soft cushions of the swing.

Papa brought Ariana a journal, too, but she tossed it aside with a laugh and pestered Papa, looking for jewelry or some other trinket. She was sorely disappointed to find that there was none to be had. She went sulking to the cliff. Sometimes she can be so unkind. I wonder how Papa will react when Mama tells him that Ariana has been visiting Widow Hobbs. Papa forbade her to go to the widow's cottage, but Ariana has never been one to listen to what is good for her. I'm not sure why Papa and Mama don't like the Widow Hobbs. She just seems like a lonely old woman who lives in a cottage at the edge of the bog. I'm sure they have their reasons, but I don't see the harm in visiting a lonely soul.

The first entry ended with an amateurish flourish of the pen. Reagan smiled to herself, remembering the awkward flourishes she used to draw under her name when she signed birthday cards to her mom. Some things must be shared between generations.

She heard footsteps on the porch and looked up. Willow was walking toward her with a strange look on her face.

"Whatcha got there?" she asked, her voice sounding strained.

"As if you don't know," accused Reagan.

"What are you talking about? Where did you get that book?"

"That's exactly what I want to know," demanded Reagan. "I want to know who put this in my room."

"Maybe you'd better slow down, not be so hostile, and tell me what you are talking about," said Willow, steadily.

"I was in my room looking at the old photo album. I came down to the kitchen to get some milk, then went back upstairs to get my library book. When I was leaving my room, I saw this book on the rocking chair. It wasn't there five minutes before because I was sitting in that very rocker. I want to know who is screwing with me and why!" Reagan's voice was pitching up, and it was obvious she was getting more and more upset.

"Please let me see the book," said Willow, softly. Reagan passed the journal to her. She carefully looked at the cover and then opened it to the first page, paling slightly.

"So, who put Adelaide's journal in my room?" asked Reagan again.

"Humph. I don't know, but I know I didn't do it. Probably Cora Rose, just messing with you. She does enjoy it so."

"She's not here to do that."

"Of course, she's here," said Willow.

"She hasn't left already?"

"No, she was staying later to pick cherries in the old orchard. She wants to preserve a bunch of them, and she'll probably make a pie or two. Those are not to be missed, Cora Rose's cherry pies. I wouldn't get my panties in a bunch about Cora Rose and her pranks. If you get upset, it will just encourage her to do even more. Just ignore it and it'll go away. I am driving into town to get some pizza. Do you want to come? If so, put your shoes on and come on." Startled by Willow's quick change of subject and rare offer of some public social time, Reagan jumped up out of the swing.

"Just let me put this away and run a brush through my hair. I'll be right out." Reagan ran up to her room and placed the journal carefully on the dressing table, swiped a brush through her hair, and ran down to meet Willow. She would deal with Cora Rose later.

That night, Reagan settled into bed with her library book. Adelaide's journal lay on the dressing table in line with the brush and Reagan's perfume. She had had enough of all the unexplained happenings. She tried to talk to Willow about it over pizza that night, but Willow shrugged it off and stuffed her face with the steaming hot pie. Reagan couldn't tell if Willow believed the house was haunted or not. Sometimes she said things that made Reagan think Willow was one of the crazies, and other times Reagan thought Willow was just messing with her to see how much Reagan would fall for. Well, it didn't matter. There were no such things as ghosts, and houses weren't haunted. On the other hand, there were a whole lot of people who were bat-shit crazy. Reagan looked down at Wiley stretched out next to her bed... and dogs, too. Dogs were bat-shit crazy, too.

Reagan woke. It was still night, and the moonlight helped to light the room. She heard a creaking sound and turned her head, looking at the rocking chair in the corner. Adelaide sat in the rocking chair, her golden hair spilling over her shoulders. Her head was bent down, and she was holding the journal in one hand and Reagan's hairbrush in the other. She was rocking slightly, and her shoulders were shaking. Reagan blinked and looked again. Adelaide was still there. It looked as though she was weeping. The journal was opened toward the last pages. Wiley sat next to her, anxiously licking the hand that held the brush. This can't be happening, Reagan thought. I have to be dreaming. She sat up in bed. Adelaide raised her head and steadied her tear-stained eyes at Reagan. She smiled a wistful smile and vanished into a swirl of mist. The journal dropped to the seat of the rocking chair, and the hairbrush fell to the floor with a clatter.

Reagan began to shake. She didn't just see that. It didn't just happen. Wiley whined at the rocking chair, then tucked his tail between his legs. He turned and looked at Reagan sitting up in bed. Wagging, he approached her and licked her hand. Reagan still stared at the chair, trembling. Wiley jumped up and placed his front paws on the bed. He gently licked her chin. When she still didn't respond, he pulled his back legs, one after another up on the bed and curled next to her. With one front paw, he gently nudged her back down on the bed until she was curled up against him, her face buried in his neck. With one paw touching her, guarding her, they both fell asleep.

CHAPTER 14

*R*eagan woke abruptly to sun streaming through her windows. The room was cheerful, and a cool breeze was bringing in the scent of the ocean. Despite the beautiful morning, Reagan felt cranky and out of sorts. She'd had crazy dreams during the night, and she didn't feel well this morning.

Wiley was stretched out next to her in the bed, his muzzle sharing her pillow. His pink tongue reached out and kissed her face. She moved toward him and snuggled into his warm fur. She didn't feel like facing the morning, and she was seriously out of sorts. The smell of coffee and bacon reminded her of Cora Rose and the conversation Reagan was planning to have with her. Thinking of Cora Rose reminded her of the dream she had the night before. Involuntarily, she glanced over at the rocking chair. Of course. The journal was on the seat and her hairbrush was on the floor. Just like in the dream. Only Cora Rose wasn't in the dream. Adelaide was.

Reagan sighed. She didn't know what to think anymore. Maybe she was the one who was going crazy. Maybe none of this was really happening, but her mind was playing tricks on her. Aren't the teen years when psychosis and other mental illnesses surface? Isn't that what she learned in the Intro. to Psych. class she took last year? What if she really was losing it?

Wiley whined and pawed her gently, licking her chin again. He knew she was stressed out. Reagan rubbed his ears gently. "Don't worry, Wiley," she whispered. "I'm made of stronger stuff than this. This crap isn't going to get to me. There's a logical explanation for everything that's happening, and I am going to find out what it is."

With a firm resolve, Reagan got out of bed. She picked up her hairbrush from the floor, brushed her hair, and set it back on the dressing table. Then she retrieved the journal from the rocking chair and put it next to the brush. She made her bed, kicking Wiley off first, then took a long hot shower, preparing herself for a confrontation with Cora Rose and to find some answers.

Cora Rose's back was to Reagan when she entered the kitchen. Reagan poured herself a cup of coffee and walked over to the cook as she was spooning scrambled eggs into a serving dish.

"Good morning, Cora Rose."

"Good morning," Cora Rose grunted in return.

"So, what is your plan today? How do you plan on messing with me? Are you going to plant a picture for me to find, or a letter? Are you going to rearrange my room so I think someone or something has been in there?" Reagan calmly helped herself to some bacon and eggs. Cora Rose turned and looked at her, hostility radiating from her eyes.

"Little missy, I don't know what you are talking about, but I don't appreciate your tone, and I really don't appreciate you accusing me of things I don't do. I don't know what crawled up your ass today, but I am not going to put up with it. If things are moving in your room or appearing in front of you, well that's because this house wants it to happen. It will happen whether you or I want it to or not. It will happen whether or not you or I believe in it. I don't really give a rat's ass if you accept it, but I am tired of your high and mighty attitude. Now, I have to feed you, but I don't have to like it, and I don't have to talk to you, thank you very much."

With that Cora Rose slammed down a hot cherry cobbler and marched out of the kitchen. Reagan stood with her mouth hanging open. She expected Cora Rose to admit she had been pranking Reagan all along. She did not expect this vitriol.

"Now you went and did it!" Reagan looked up to see Willow coming into the kitchen. "Reagan, you need to watch your mouth and your attitude. You came here not understanding the superstitions and beliefs of a small, historic community. You insult the person who feeds you every day and cleans your room, and you don't even stop to consider that what she believes is part of her heritage or the fabric of her soul. I told you to let it be, but you just couldn't, could you? Now I have to make sure I don't lose the best damn breakfast cook in the county." With that, Willow stalked out of the kitchen looking for Cora Rose.

Tears sprung to Reagan's eyes. She considered dumping the breakfast on her plate into the trash because she no longer felt like eating, but then she realized that would be an even greater insult to Cora Rose. Meekly, she made her way to the kitchen table, sat down with her steaming plate, and began to choke down her food. Tears ran silently down her checks as she wept and ate. She felt incredibly alone. She missed her mom, she didn't feel like she belonged with Willow and Cora Rose, and even Wiley wasn't next to her right now. With a sob, she lay her head down on the table next to her eggs and just lost it.

As all the frustration and stress of the last couple of weeks poured out of her eyes and onto the table, Reagan felt a soft touch stroke the top of her head. Light fingers pulled a strand of hair that was stuck to the tears on her cheek and tucked it behind her ears. Reagan didn't move, soaking in the moment of compassion. She didn't realize Willow had it in her to be empathetic, but apparently, she did. Taking a shaky, steadying breath, Reagan raised her head just as Cora Rose and Willow walked into the kitchen, followed by a subdued Wiley. Then Reagan broke down completely.

"Girl, what the hell is wrong with you today? Are you having your monthly or something?" Cora Rose stared at the sobbing girl at the table. "Stop that nonsense and eat your food before it gets cold. Just because you are having a hard time accepting things you don't understand isn't a good enough reason to waste my good cooking, and I have to tell you, I did a damn fine job on the cherry cobbler if I have to say so myself."

"Yes, you did, Cora Rose," said Willow as she stuffed a second forkful into her mouth. "This is damn delicious. Probably the best you have ever made. Don't wait too long to taste it, Reagan. You'll want to eat it while it's hot. Cora Rose, do we have any fresh cream to pour on this?"

Reagan raised her head from the table and swiped at her eyes. She was astounded that these two were going on as if nothing had happened. Cora Rose set down a small pitcher of cream, and Willow proceeded to pour it calmly over her hot cobbler. Reagan's breath came in a loud, shaky hiccup sound, and Willow and Cora Rose laughed.

"I'm really sorry Cora Rose. I just thought you were pranking me over and over again, I was just getting tired of it. I don't know what is happening. I don't understand it, and I just can't wrap my head around it being something, I don't know, supernatural or something."

"Then don't wrap your head around it. Just let it be. Continue on with your life, and just let it be. Do you understand how monarch butterflies can migrate all the way to Mexico? Those delicate, fragile beauties can take a trip for 3,000 miles and not get lost. Do you think about that? Do you understand how they do it? Yet, do you doubt that they do it?" Reagan shook her head 'no.' "Do you know how bees can tell other bees how to find an amazing field filled with pollen? Do you know how chameleons can change their color to blend into their surroundings? All of these miracles, all of these unexplained things, do you stop your day to think about them? Does it affect you in any way?" Again, Reagan shook her head. "Then why can you not look at this in the same way? There is something that you don't understand. This is just one of life's mysteries. Let it go and coexist."

"I hear what you're saying, but Willow, someone or something touched me just now. I felt someone smoothing down my hair and comforting me. At first I thought it was you."

"Yeah, right!" said Willow. Reagan laughed.

"Well, I have to admit. It did surprise me that you would do that, but who else could it have been? Then I looked up and saw you two coming into the kitchen."

"Probably Adelaide," said Cora Rose. "She is the nice one. Was she humming?"

"No, she was quiet. But last night, I swear I saw her in my room. She was in the rocking chair, holding my brush and her journal. She was crying. Then she vanished. This morning, my brush was on the floor and the journal was on the rocking chair where it fell from her hand."

"Adelaide won't harm you, dear. She probably uses your brush every night. They say she was pretty damn vain about that hair of hers," said Willow. "She is beautiful, naïve, but kind. You have nothing to fear if you encounter Adelaide. Nothing at all. Okay, so if you two aren't going to kill each other, and Cora Rose is going to continue in my employ, then I can go to work. Deal?" Reagan nodded, and Cora Rose humphed.

Willow took that for a yes and left the kitchen on the way to the barn. Reagan looked up meekly at Cora Rose and apologized again.

"I feel terrible, Cora Rose. I am really sorry. On the other hand, this cherry cobbler is really amazing."

Cora Rose beamed in spite of herself and started humming as she began to clean the kitchen. Reagan finished her breakfast, rolled up her sleeves and helped Cora Rose finish the clean-up.

When they finished, Reagan told Cora Rose that she was going to go down to the ocean for a bit, but later was going into town, did she need anything? Cora Rose thought for a minute but then said she was good. As Reagan was walking out the door, Cora Rose called her back.

"What Willow said was true," Cora Rose began. "Adelaide won't cause you any harm, but there are other things that will. Despite the fact that you think I'm crazy, you need to be very careful of the wolves under that table, and whatever you do, don't go up on the fourth floor." Reagan swallowed her initial reply and muttered a 'yes ma'am' and a 'thank you,' and walked out of the house with Wiley close on her heels.

REAGAN MADE her way down the cliff trail and onto the rocks. The tide was out, and the gulls were preoccupied with the bounty left in the rock crevices. They paid no attention to her today. She heard a soft whistling and saw Seth rounding the cliff, walking toward her with a smile on his face. Clasped in his left hand was a fistful of wildflowers. As he reached Reagan, he extended his hand presenting her the bouquet.

"Thanks," stammered Reagan. "Why do I deserve this?"

"I kind of figured you might need cheering up today," said Seth. "How's your head? Any serious damage from yesterday's gull attack?"

"I think I'll live," said Reagan. Seth smiled and grabbed her hand, pulling her down to sit on the rocks next to him.

"I have something else for you," he said. He pulled out a clean cloth handkerchief and unfolded it. Nestled in the soft white fabric was a small, black metal starfish pendant hung on an intricately knotted string necklace. The starfish had a delicate pattern, and the black metal glowed with a burnished waxed finish. It was exquisite and primitive, and it looked vaguely familiar.

"This is for me?" asked Reagan. "It's beautiful. This is obviously expensive. I can't take it."

"Expensive? No, I made it." Seth said, modestly.

"You made this? You mean you knotted the string to make the chain?"

"Yes, I did that, but I also made the starfish."

"Are you kidding? How did you do that?"

"I make a lot of things. We often need things for the boat and the household. We make what we need when we need it. At one time, the place where you live was a working farm. They had the ability and the tools they needed to make whatever they required." Reagan thought of all the rooms on the first-floor basement. She remembered seeing the baskets half-finished and the butchering room.

"That's pretty awesome. I can't do anything. My aunt makes beautiful pottery, and you make beautiful things out of metal, but all I ever do is read. I don't have a creative bone in my body. I love this starfish. Even though it is metal, it feels warm."

"Here, let me tie it on for you." Reagan lifted the necklace to her neck and Seth swept her hair to the side and over her shoulder. His fingers lingered on the back of her neck before they slid down the hank of hair. A gull cried overhead and began to circle them. Another joined them. Reagan tensed, but Seth shushed her. "It'll be fine."

A gull swooped, and Reagan ducked. Quickly, Seth tied the knotted string chain and kissed the spot where it fell against her skin. The gulls screamed. Reagan was sure they sounded angry. One swooped close but stopped in mid-flight and veered away. Seth kissed her cheek, his eyes cast toward the sky in defiance.

The gulls cried out in frustration but wouldn't come close. "The starfish will protect you," Seth whispered. "Keep it on, and you'll be safe." Reagan laughed at the serious note in his voice.

"I love the sentiment, and I think it's sweet, so I will wear it because you gave it to me, but not because I think it has magical powers."

"I don't care what you think, I just care that you wear it. Think of it as part of me. I made it, so it has some of my spirit. It will be there when I can't, and it will keep you safe."

He looked deep in her eyes, and she felt a chill. She wasn't sure if it was because of the words he spoke, or just because of the strange way he was looking at her. As soon as it came, the chill passed. Then she felt a flush of warmth and quickly looked away. She realized she was staring at him hungrily, obvious that she wanted him to kiss her. He laughed and delightedly obliged while gulls flew in circles over their heads crying loudly.

Reagan closed her eyes and let herself get swept away. Seth's cool lips tasted vaguely of the ocean. Her heart beat rapidly in her chest as his fingers twisted in her hair. He pulled her closer to him and kissed her deeply. She sighed and leaned into him.

The starfish that now lay on her chest seemed to warm her. She broke away from his lips and looked into his eyes. They were a soft gray-blue today, darker than before, but lit with a fiery glow. He groaned and drew her close again. She lay her head on his chest.

Suddenly, she felt compelled to look up the cliff toward the house. It was like she was being watched. Half expecting Willow or Cora Rose to be peering down over the cliff edge, she was relieved to see that the trail above her was empty. Then she glanced up higher, to the old house. Her eyes traveled over the windows of the fourth floor until she came to the corner room, the room with the rounded windows that formed a tower at the corner of the house.

Then she saw her. A shadowy figure in a long dress, dark

tangled tresses and eyes that bore into Reagan's soul. She stiffened. Seth pulled back and looked at her pale face. Then he followed her stare to the window of the tower room. His eyes locked with the eyes of the shadow lady, and his lips quirked up quickly in a little grin. The image of the woman vanished. Then he looked down at Reagan.

"What's wrong?" he asked her.

"Did you see her? Did you see that woman?"

"What woman?" he asked her.

"The woman in the window. In the curved window of the tower on the fourth floor. Didn't you see her?"

"I don't see anything now, do you?" Reagan looked at the window and saw nothing, just the reflection of some clouds and the gulls that filled the sky.

"No, there's nothing there. Just my imagination running away with me. These damn gulls have me spooked."

"I told you, you're safe with me. You have nothing to worry about," said Seth as he touched the starfish pendant with his index finger. Then he lifted the finger to her lips. She kissed it. He pressed it to his mouth, then stood. He kissed the top of her warm head and walked away, disappearing around the curve of the cliff, just like he did every time he left her.

CHAPTER 15

*R*eagan leaned back against the rocks and basked in the memory of Seth's kiss. She didn't know a thing about this man, but she loved how he made her feel. He always seemed to know when she was coming down to the rocks, but he never stayed long. For a moment, her heart skipped a beat.

How did he always know when she was going to be on the cliffs? Was he stalking her? Not liking the creepy thought, she pushed it aside. He hadn't done anything to make her nervous. He seemed like a serious guy, more mature than the boys back home. Probably because he worked on the fishing boat with his dad. It was like he was more centered and responsible than other kids his age. She also had the impression he wasn't a rich kid, but rather had to work for the things he had.

Who did she know who could make a starfish necklace like the one he made her? She reached up to touch the pendant that now hung around her neck. No one she knew would even have a clue how to begin to make something like that. She loved the little black starfish, but something about it bothered her. It was almost like she had seen it before, but where? She remembered the starfish she had seen in the tide pool the first time she had met

Seth. Maybe that is what she was thinking about. It was a remarkable likeness.

She closed her eyes and thought about the morning. She really had been a brat to Cora Rose. It wasn't like her to be rude and inconsiderate. Maybe she really was under some stress. She enjoyed living at the cliff house and spending her summer reading, but she missed her mom, and she missed being a normal teenager. She wasn't used to being cooped up and not going to the mall or a movie or something. She probably needed some kind of companionship. She wished she would have asked Seth if he wanted to go into town or something, but he was long gone, and she wasn't the type to go chasing after a boy. Maybe she could text Olivia and see if she wanted to do anything.

Pulling out her cell phone, she sent a quick text to her mom letting her know she was okay and that she missed her. Then she texted Olivia saying she was bored and wanted to hang out, was there anything to do in this sleepy town? She gazed out at the ocean, watching a pod of dolphins playing in the waves while waiting for a response from either one of the texts. The first came from her mom. She was well, and she was glad that Reagan was doing okay. There was a chance that her assignment might be shorter than expected, so she might get home sooner than they had anticipated. That made Reagan smile, and she texted her mom that although she was having a good time, she would be happy to be going home early. Her mom cautioned her not to count on it, but just wanted to give her a heads up.

Still grinning at the thought of a shortened time in Maine, another text came through. This one was from Olivia. She couldn't do anything today because she was canning cherries with her mom, but she and her friends were planning on going to Orchard Bend Beach the next day if Reagan wanted to tag along. Reagan let her know she was interested and asked her to be sure to send the details. Then she headed up the cliff to return to the house.

Reagan went up to her room to grab her car keys and her purse. Her brush was right where she left it, and the journal was also still next to the brush. Nothing had been moved. She gathered her library books and left a note in the kitchen for Willow that she was driving into town and to call her if she needed anything.

Reagan stopped at the drugstore and picked up a new bottle of shampoo. As she headed toward the cashier, she passed a display of handcrafted soaps; the sign touting the maker as a local soap artisan. The heady aromas made Reagan pause and pick up each different bar of soap, inhaling and appreciating their individual fragrances and beautiful swirled colors. Each bar was hand cut and unwrapped, the silky-smooth texture imparted moisture to Reagan's dry fingertips. Selecting one called Blueberry Delight, Reagan lifted it to her nose.

"That's my favorite," a deep voice spoke behind her. Startled, Reagan almost dropped the bar. "I'm sorry. I didn't mean to scare you."

"It's okay. I didn't see you behind me. So, Blueberry Delight is your favorite?" quipped Reagan with her eyebrow raised as she took in the tall, dark-haired guy standing in front of her. "You bathe with Blueberry Delight?" He grinned unabashedly back at her.

"I do. I am also very fond of Bay Rum and Warm Vanilla. I don't like Lemon Dream though." Not sure if he was pulling her leg, Reagan glanced over her shoulder at the soap display. Sure enough, Bay Rum and Warm Vanilla were there, although there was a short supply of the Bay Rum. The Lemon Dream stack was plentiful. She picked up the Bay Rum and smelled it. It was warm and masculine, and reminded her slightly of Seth's scent, although his was spicier and carried more citrus.

"Okay, so you like handmade artisan soaps. That's cool," Reagan responded, flirting a little.

"Well, I can't help but like them. My mom makes them, and I

am often corralled to help," said the still grinning young man. "So, hello. I'm Chase Renault. My mom has been making soap since I was a baby, and her mother made it before her. I suppose all my ancestors made their own soap at one time because no one bought it at the store, but Mom makes the good smelling stuff that's good for your skin... yada, yada, yada."

"I can't argue with you. It smells amazing." Reagan dropped the bar of Blueberry Delight into her shopping cart. "Do you always just hang out by the soap display, promoting your mom's business?"

"Nope, I work here, stocking shelves and stuff. You haven't told me your name, so I guess you don't want me to know it, you're painfully shy, or just incredibly rude," said Chase. Reagan's face instantly colored a deep red, and she began to sputter. "Relax. I am just messing with you. I know who you are. Your name is Reagan, and you're Willow's niece. All the kids in town think you are either crazy or incredibly brave to be living out at Willow's place."

"And what do you think, Chase? Crazy or brave?"

"Neither."

"What do you mean? Don't you share the town's fascination with my aunt's house and the fact that it is haunted or whatever."

"Do you believe it's haunted?" asked Chase.

"No, I don't believe in that stuff," said Reagan, but she flashed back on the scene this morning with the journal and the hairbrush and the subsequent blow up with Cora Rose.

"You seemed to hesitate there. Do you believe, yes, or no?"

"Definitely, no," declared Reagan. "How about you? Do you believe?"

"Of course, I do. I live in Littleport, don't I?" asked Chase. Chase looked at her steadily with that grin still planted on his face. Wow, he was good looking, but damn, everyone here was crazy. Nothing had changed.

"You look disappointed. Did you want me to say I didn't believe in that stuff?"

"Yes, I did, actually. I would like to meet just one person here who isn't bat-shit crazy." The words were out of her mouth before she had a chance to think about what she was going to say. Her face turned an even deeper red. "Oh, my goodness. I am so sorry. I didn't mean..."

"Yes, you did," said Chase, but remarkably, he didn't look angry, just amused. "You aren't from around here, you don't feel like you belong, and everyone here talks crazy about ghosts and spirits. I can't say I blame you. But don't think of me as the bat-shit crazy type. Think of me as the maybe there are things we can't explain type, but I don't think that the world is a Stephen King novel."

"So, you don't believe in the wolves under the dining room tables kind of spirits?" asked Reagan. Chase let out a laugh, deep and hearty.

"Cora Rose is at it again," he chuckled. "Is she filling your head with the terrors of attack wolves in Willow's dining room? She has told that story to anyone who will listen."

"But people do listen, don't they?"

"Hell, yes!" exclaimed Chase.

"Why?"

"Because she is the best damn cook in all of Littleport, and if she likes you and you'll listen to her stories, she'll bring you a fresh blueberry pie. There is not a soul in this town who doesn't welcome Cora Rose onto their front porch for a spell of good ghost story talk if it means they will be rewarded with a fresh, hot pie. You should know, I expect you have sampled a lot of her cooking since you have been staying with Willow."

"That I have, and you're right, she is an amazing cook, but I will suffer for it before too long." Reagan looked down at her flat tummy and patted it. "My hips are going to be twice their size by the time summer is over." Chase's gaze lingered on Reagan's hips, sliding up slowly to her face.

"I don't think you have to worry in that department," said Chase. Again, Reagan blushed furiously.

"Um, well, thanks." With that, Reagan moved toward the cash register. Chase slipped behind the counter and totaled her purchases.

"So, I'm off in half an hour, do you want to hang out or something?" asked Chase.

"I'm headed over to the library after this. Stop by and see if I'm still there. If I am, then maybe... or maybe not," said Reagan coyly. She picked up her purchases and left the drugstore.

Stowing her soap in her car, she retrieved her books and walked across the square to the library. Dropping her books in the return slot, Reagan turned and headed to the shelves which held the detective and mystery novels. She was devouring books quickly, so she wanted to select several that would hold her for the week.

It took her about fifteen minutes to pick out four novels, then she meandered her way through the shelves. She ended up in the non-fiction section. She was never good with the Dewey Decimal System, so she just read the titles, looking at the various topics, seeing if anything sparked her interest. Reagan looked at some cooking books, wondering if she might want to try some recipes, but then she thought about how Cora Rose might take it and she moved quickly on. She found the craft section and scanned the shelves for soap making. She was curious about what was involved in making that silky, amazing smelling bar that was in her car. Flipping through a couple of books, she decided that it was way too long and complicated a process if you made everything from scratch.

Wandering some more, she recognized that she was just killing time until Chase got off work. She was craving some social time, and Chase might just fit the bill. As she mused about the possibilities that Chase might offer, she noticed a group of books on the shelf in front of her.

One book was pulled slightly out from the others as if someone had looked at it, but shelved it hastily, not shoving it in all the way. The title of the book was *Hauntings, Unexplained Happenings, and Undeniable Truths.* Curious, Reagan slid the book off the shelf. She leaned against the stacks and thumbed her way through the pages. Fuzzy photographs and pen and ink sketches littered the pages, along with old houses, abandoned barns, and broken windows with ghostly auras.

Before she knew it, she was caught up in an old tale of a young girl who was put off a wagon in the middle of the night, abandoned by her family, too poor to be able to feed another mouth. The child wandered the road, following the wagon as long as she could. Exhausted, cold, and hungry, she turned to follow a railroad track assuming it would lead her to a town and to people who would help her.

Inexperienced, she was unaware of the dangers of walking the tracks. She stumbled in her exhaustion, and her tiny foot slipped and wedged under a rail. Unable to free herself, an early morning train struck and killed her, the engineer never seeing the child. Even if he'd had a warning, he wouldn't have been able to slow down.

Her body was found by a farmer the next day, flung a hundred feet from the track. Her little foot was found still wedged under the rail. An investigation was conducted, and someone remembered a family passing through with numerous small children, the parents inquiring if anyone needed a young girl to act as a servant. Unable to find the family, no one was charged.

The child was laid to rest in an unmarked grave. No one stepped up to pay the expenses of a marker stone, and the incident was forgotten until an old farmer was driving his load of hay into town to be delivered to the livery stable. He was flagged down by a young girl in a dirty and torn green gingham dress. She had a pronounced limp. As he helped her into his wagon to give her a ride to town, he couldn't help but notice that her right leg was missing a foot. Feeling frightened, but chastising himself for having the willies, he climbed up into the wagon and urged his horses forward in a fast trot. He turned to speak to the girl, but she had vanished, no sign of her anywhere. Fearing she had fallen out of the wagon, he stopped his team and climbed back down. Checking the road carefully and peering under the wagon, he searched in vain for the little girl. According to the book, stories like this had been reported for years, and people to this day continue to report seeing a little girl in a tattered green dress standing by the road near the tracks.

"I thought you said you didn't believe in ghost stuff and implied that anyone who did was, how did you put it, 'bat-shit crazy'." Chase's voice sounded behind her.

"You like sneaking up on people, don't you?"

"Yep, it's kind of fun to watch them jump. So, did curiosity just happen to get the better of you, or did you really intend to come and do some research but didn't want to admit it?"

"No, I came to get some more novels to read, and I just started scanning the shelves. I found this book and was curious. I really hadn't even thought of doing research. It seems silly to research things that aren't real."

"Maybe you could become enlightened. Open your mind to what other people believe. You may have to weed through the obviously ignorant and fake stuff, but I bet you could find some things that are hard to explain. You might also understand why people actually believe some of the stuff you find so hard to. Does that seem fair to you? It's got to help you understand Cora Rose better and maybe earn you some pie." Reagan shrugged and looked up into his earnest brown eyes.

"You're serious, aren't you?"

"There's nothing wrong with educating yourself so you can

make sound decisions. You never know, you may become a believer."

"Fat chance," Reagan quipped, but she tucked the book in her elbow with the detective novels she was eager to read.

"So, despite the fact that you think I am a crackpot, can I convince you to go have a malt with me?"

"I'll reserve judgment on the crackpot but take you up on the malt." Reagan checked out her books and she and Chase walked them to Reagan's car. As she opened the door, the scent of Blueberry Delight spilled out. "I may have to buy another bar just to use as an air freshener. The stuff smells amazing. I looked in a book at how to make soap since I had never heard of anyone who did that. The process seems long and complicated."

"It is, but like anything, once you get used to it, it's not a big deal. You should stop by and watch my mom someday. I know she would love it. She likes it when people are interested in her craft."

"I would love to."

They walked over to the diner and both ordered chocolate malts. Sitting at a table by the window, they settled in and got to know each other. Chase was a junior in high school, a pole vaulter, and was working at the drug store to save money for college. He had an easy way of talking about himself, not self-conscious in any way.

Reagan filled him in on her mom's job reporting on the troops overseas, and her subsequent visit to Maine. Reagan was shocked when she discovered she had already finished her malt. The time had passed easily between them. Reagan reached for her check, but Chase stopped her.

"I invited you for malts, remember?"

"Thank you, but I can pay for my own. This wasn't like a date or anything." Reagan explained.

"In this town, if a guy invites a girl, he pays. We're old-fashioned like that." Reagan opened her mouth to speak, but Chase interrupted her. "Don't get your feminist panties in a bunch. It wasn't a sexist remark, just a matter of etiquette. If you ask me out, I will gladly let you pay, deal?"

"Deal, but I don't have feminist panties. I'm not sure if I should be insulted because I'm a female, or if I should just laugh because you're ridiculous."

"You should laugh. Life is too serious to get your undies twisted about anything so trivial. I've got this. I also will pay for the movie tickets and popcorn tomorrow night." Reagan looked at him with her mouth hanging open.

"You're incredibly sure of yourself, aren't you?"

"Yep. You noticed that you didn't say no, right?" Reagan laughed and blushed. They exchanged contact information, and as Reagan left the diner, she decided that she had just had the most productive day yet since moving in with Willow.

CHAPTER 16

"A re you coming?" asked Olivia, as she drug the cooler across the sand.

"Right behind you," said Reagan as she struggled with the armload of beach blankets and a tote that was threatening to slide off of her left shoulder.

"It's not much further, just over this last dune," said Olivia. Reagan followed her dutifully wondering why this section of beach, which was the furthest from the parking lot, was better than the closer sections. As she crested the top of the dune, her question was answered. This part of the beach was practically deserted, expect for the small group of teenagers setting up beach umbrellas and coolers. If she looked to her left, she could see that the beach closer to the lot was full of moms and their children. The squeals of delight reached Reagan's ears as small children ran to escape the licking waves. Although the happy sounds made her smile, she was glad that they were in a more deserted and private area.

"Hi guys," said Olivia. "This is Reagan. Reagan, this is everybody. You know Darcy over there." Darcy smiled, but there wasn't a lot of warmth in it. That didn't bother Reagan. If Darcy wanted to be a bitch, then so be it. "This is Savannah and Maria, and those two goofballs are Todd and Dale. Hey Darcy, where is Tom?"

"He had to finish helping his dad roof Mr. Rainer's shed." Her pretty lips were turned down in a pout. It was obvious she wasn't happy to be without her boyfriend. "He said he would try to come out later, but if he doesn't, it's his loss." She tossed her head, trying to act indifferent, but she wasn't fooling anyone.

Olivia and Reagan set up their blanket and cooler and slapped on a generous portion of sunscreen. Darcy looked over curiously.

"So how is it going over at Willow's house? Anything creepy or weird?" said Darcy. Olivia shot Darcy a warning look.

"I've settled in fairly well. I was having trouble sleeping in a new place, but now I'm comfortable and sleeping like a baby."

"Well," said Darcy, "I still can't imagine living there. I wouldn't even set foot on the place and neither would anyone else here." She looked around for affirmation. Savannah and Maria nodded their heads slightly, but to give them credit, they did look slightly embarrassed. Todd and Dale just looked on curiously.

"Well, I spent the afternoon there with Reagan and nothing happened except I got to see inside a really cool old house. It's full of beautiful antiques, and there is an unlimited Pepsi supply in the fridge," said Olivia, nonchalantly. Darcy's mouth dropped open, and Savannah stifled a giggle. The boys grinned at the fact that Darcy was speechless. They jumped up from their blankets and set up the volleyball net. Within minutes, the whole group was batting a ball around on the beach, and Reagan was content to be in the company of teenagers, even if one of them was Darcy.

Later, after munching on a sandwich, Reagan stood up and pulled on her cover up. She gathered her things and stuffed them in her tote.

"Where are you going?" asked Olivia, as she lazily rolled from her back to her tummy.

"I've got to go home and take a shower. I'm going to the movies tonight with Chase."

"Wait, what? You have a date with Chase? Chase Renault?"

Reagan nodded, absently searching for her left flip flop. "Yeah, why?"

"When did this happen? When did you meet him? How did you get him to take you out?" Olivia hammered her with questions.

"I met him at the drugstore. We had a conversation. I went to the library. We got a malt. He asked me to the movies. End of story. What is the big deal?"

"The big deal is Chase Renault doesn't go out. Every female in Littleport has wanted to go out with him, but he doesn't bite. Not even Darcy has managed to catch him," said Savannah.

"I shamelessly flirted with him two years ago," sighed Maria. "He was nice and polite, but that was it. We all wondered if he was gay."

"He probably is," said Darcy coyly.

"Well, we're just going to a movie, so I don't think it matters one way or another if he is gay, and if it turns out he isn't, you guys will never know, because I don't kiss and tell," laughed Reagan. "I'll see you later. Olivia, thanks for inviting me. I will call you tomorrow." With that, Reagan walked over the dune smiling to herself. *I really don't think the boy is gay,* she thought to herself, *and I have a hunch I might find out the answer to that question tonight.*

REAGAN WAS SITTING on the front porch, swinging gently in the suspended porch swing, totally immersed in her current read when Wiley scrambled to his feet, his tail wagging. Reagan looked around but didn't see what had Wiley's attention. Then he hopped down the porch steps, his butt wiggling in anticipation. Reagan got up from the swing and looked down the driveway. She didn't see a thing, but Wiley was excited about something. A second later, a car emerged from the trees that lined the lower section of the drive. The car stopped at the front of the barn and Chase got out.

"Hey Wiley, how ya doin' fella? Hang on, get your nose out of my pocket. You know I have a treat for you, don't cha, buddy."

"Obviously, Wiley knows you. I didn't realize you knew him."

"Sure, I know Wiley. My mom has me deliver stuff and puppy biscuits here all the time."

"Puppy biscuits?"

"Sure, my mom makes homemade puppy biscuits, organic with good for dog herbs and stuff. Wiley likes them. Willow said she thought they tasted pretty good."

"They do taste good. Hey Chase, what brings you out here today? Is your mom okay? Does she need anything?" asked Willow, as she came out of the barn.

"No, Mom is fine. She says hello. I came to take Reagan out to a movie if that's okay?"

"I suppose that would be okay. I'm guessing you are trustworthy."

"Excuse me. I'm standing right here. I think I can decide when I go out and with whom, who, whom… or whatever."

"Calm down, tiger," said Chase. "I keep having to explain village life to the girl," Chase said, teasing.

"Ooh, you two are annoying. Maybe the two of you should go out."

"Ya wanna come, Willow?" asked Chase. Willow's eyes twinkled. She was enjoying watching the normally confident Reagan squirm.

"Hmmm, I haven't been to a movie in a long time. Might be kind of fun."

"Of course, you are welcome to come, Aunt Willow. I just thought you had soooo much work to do, with that giant order, and all," said Reagan, sweetly.

"All work and no play makes Willow a dull girl, but you're right. I do have a lot of work. Please be careful and don't stay out too late. Chase, you be certain to walk Reagan to the door when you drop her off tonight. Do you understand me?" Willow gazed steadily at Chase, and he nodded slightly. Reagan looked at the two of them aware that some silent communication had just passed between them and she wasn't included.

"Don't worry, Willow, I am a big girl and not afraid of the bogey man. I've told you that."

"Yes, but I told you that I have been raised a gentleman, and I will walk you to the door and make sure you're locked in safely. Humor your Aunt Willow. After all, the older generation is set in their ways." Willow swatted at Chase.

"Come on Wiley. Let the young folk go play. You come on in and keep me company."

Chase tossed another biscuit to Wiley and opened the passenger door for Reagan.

"Are you ready to go?"

"Let me put my book away and grab my purse. Do you mind waiting?"

Reagan closed the door and waited to turn off the porch light, making sure Chase could see his way back to his car. She hugged herself and smiled. She had a wonderful evening. Chase was easy and relaxed and fun to be around. He wasn't like a lot of guys who try to impress everyone around them. He was the poster child for laid back. It didn't even feel like they were on their first date. After the first half hour, it felt like they were old friends.

The movie was a romantic comedy and had a feel-good ending. When it was over, they grabbed some coffee and went for a walk along the deserted beach.

Chase talked easily about himself. Like Reagan, his dad had passed away when he was young. His mom worked at her cottage industry creating soaps, herbal lotions, and other healing products. He took his studies seriously, and he was hoping for a scholarship or two to help him pay for college.

Reagan mentioned that Darcy and Savannah said that he didn't date. She left out the part that there was speculation that he was gay. He had looked at her sideways and told her that no one had sparked his interest until just recently. Then he reached over and took her hand in his, and they walked down the beach watching the moon's reflection on the water.

When he dropped her off, he very politely told her goodnight, then gently kissed her on the forehead. He asked if he might see her again. It was silly and old-fashioned, and she loved it. She told him to call her when he was ready, and she was pretty sure she would be able to fit him into her schedule. Grinning, she gently closed the door on him, and now she was leaning against that door, smiling and listening to the car pull down the driveway.

"So, I take it you had a good night," said a voice in the darkness. Reagan gasped and turned around.

"You scared the shit out of me. I mean crap out of me. Why are you sitting in the dark?"

"I wasn't. You were so moon-faced over Chase that when you flipped the porch light off, you flipped the kitchen light off, too. You didn't even notice that I was sitting here with my Pepsi. You just backed in the door, watched out the window, then flipped both lights off. Either you've got it bad or you're daft."

"I had a good time. I don't 'have it bad,' and I don't think I'm daft."

"Well, that's good, now would you mind turning the kitchen light back on, please?" Reagan felt the blush rising on her face as she flipped the switch that turned on the small wall sconce light. The kitchen was bathed in a soft, warm glow from the tiny lamp.

"To be fair, Aunt Willow, this light doesn't really light up the kitchen. You are still in some shadow over there. It's not like you were sitting with the big overhead light on. I mean, you might even have been hiding out over there in those shadows, trying to make me look bad." Reagan teased. "Wait, are you eating cookies? Did Cora Rose make cookies and I missed it? What the heck?" Willow offered a soft chocolate chip cookie, and Reagan grabbed a glass of milk to go with it. They sat in a companionable silence, enjoying a late-night snack. For the first time since Reagan had arrived that summer, she actually felt comfortable and at home.

Later that evening, Reagan brushed her hair, lining up her hairbrush like she did every night, but tonight she was certain that things would still be in order when she woke up. Crawling into bed, she decided to read a page or two of Adelaide's diary before she tackled the difficult plot twists of her forensic mystery novel.

Today S. came home from the sea. He has been gone for a fortnight. He brought me a beautiful carved wooden box that he said came from some islands in the sea far south from here. S traded with an old man a carving of a whale for the box. The man told him that the box came from an exotic island and was carved by the native people who lived there. I think it is exquisite, and I will cherish it forever. Ariana said it was crude and cheap. I don't understand why she is so unkind. Papa asked where I got the box, and when I told him, he looked so cross. So far, he hasn't forbidden me to see S. but I am worried he might. I just want him to see that S. is a wonderful man. It's funny, but Ariana always has unkind things to say about him, but her eyes follow him whenever he is around. It is strange.

Reagan closed the journal. She didn't really feel a connection or care much about Adelaide's love life. It just didn't intrigue her like the suspense of a good mystery, so she put the journal aside and read her library book for the next half hour. When her eyes started to close of their own accord, she put the book on her bedside table and turned out the light. It had been a wonderful day, but she was tired. She fell into a deep sleep within minutes.

Adelaide stood on the edge of the cliff, her long hair lifting in the ocean breeze. She looked at Reagan and gestured for her to come closer. Reagan hesitated, feeling a cold ball of fear in the pit of her stomach. Frantically, Adelaide motioned for Reagan to hurry. Reagan gave in and moved toward her. The closer she got, the more she could see that Adelaide's clothes were soiled and torn. Her dress was clinging to her body, obviously drenched, and bits of seaweed clung to her hair and her skirt. Seagulls curled overhead, dive bombing Adelaide's head, striking her face. When Reagan got within an arm's length, she realized that Adelaide's eyes were missing, plucked from their sockets by a gull that had landed on her shoulder.

Reagan covered her face with her hands and screamed in terror. Something struck the top of her head; the wings of a gull. She opened her eyes for a second, and in front of her stood, not Adelaide, but Ariana, smiling triumphantly, her head thrown back and her arms raised to the sky. Reagan ducked her head and screamed again, trying to protect herself from the onslaught of attacking seagulls. She felt the wings beating her and the talons slashing toward her face. A hand closed around her neck, Ariana's hands, tightening, closing her throat, as if a noose was squeezing off all of her air. She couldn't breathe, and the gulls were tangled in her hair.

Wiley whined, pawing at the blankets. Reagan thrashed back and forth, caught up in the twisted sheet. Wiley leapt on the bed and tried to lick Reagan's face while trying to avoid her wildly thrashing arms. He whimpered again and barked softly, this time pawing at Reagan's shoulder. Her eyes flew open, wild with terror. Wiley settled down on the blankets, stretching his body alongside hers. He laid his big, bony head on her shoulder and gently licked her chin. Her breathing hitched as she tried to catch her breath and orient herself on this side of her dream world.

"Wiley, stop. I'm good. I'm awake. You are such a good dog. How did you know I was having a bad dream?" Wiley thumped his tail against the bed and looked over his shoulder at the rocking chair. Reagan was afraid to glance over, but she forced herself to. Nothing was there, and nothing was out of place. Just a stupid dream, she told herself. Nothing more. Just a really stupid dream. Still, there was something so sinister about it. She was having trouble shaking it off.

When she was a little kid, she used to have a lot of bad dreams, especially after her daddy died. Her mother would get out of bed and make Reagan a big mug of hot chocolate. It would always calm her down and help her fall back to sleep. She wished her mom were here now, and she wished she had that mug of hot chocolate clasped between her two hands, but it was just not meant to be. She was damn sure she wasn't going to go walking down to the kitchen tonight to get herself some of the hot, soothing drink. Even though she didn't believe in the wolves under the dining room table, tonight wasn't a night she was eager to test out her theory.

CHAPTER 17

*R*eagan woke up cranky and out of sorts. After the dream, she slept fitfully for the rest of the night. Wiley stayed by her side, pressed firmly up against her. He was tired and cranky, too, having watched over her while she slept. He jumped off the bed stiffly, arching his back once all four feet were on the floor. Then one by one, he stretched his hind legs straight back as far as he could with a pained look on his face.

"Poor, Wiley. You look like one sore dog. You must have had a miserable night just like I did. I'm sorry, fella." Wiley slowly wagged his tail and smiled a tired Labrador retriever smile. Suddenly, his ears perked up, hearing something to his liking downstairs. With a glance back at Reagan, as if making sure she was okay, he bounded out of the room and hurried down the stairs.

"Leaving me for a scrap dropped by Cora Rose, huh? So much for loyalty," teased Reagan. As she left the room to head for a hot shower, she checked her hairbrush. It was lined up right where it belonged. At least that was one thing going right this morning thought Reagan.

Reagan padded down the hall to the bathroom with one

thought on her mind; a hot shower. She felt miserable. After such an enjoyable evening with Chase, she didn't expect to wake up all out of sorts.

She spun the faucets, adjusting the shower to a steamy, hard stream of water. Sighing, she stepped in and let the water pound on her shoulders. One good thing about an old house, she thought to herself, there are no water saving features here. The amount of water massaging her shoulders was pure heaven. She moved so it hammered the top of her head.

She thought about last night and how much she enjoyed the time she'd spent with Chase. He was easy to hang out with and easy on the eyes. Then her thoughts moved on to Seth. He was another one who was good looking, but he left her feeling unsettled. Chase made her feel at peace, Seth stirred up all kinds of emotions. She thought of the last time they were together, the starfish he gave her, his cool lips on hers. Just thinking of that made her heart flutter. She reached up to touch the starfish around her neck, but there was nothing hanging there. She suffered a moment of panic.

What could have happened to it? She was certain she had it on last night. She remembered reaching up and touching it when she started walking on the beach with Chase. Even though she didn't believe in its protective powers, she still felt the comfort of it laying nestled in the hollow between her collar bones. She never took it off because Seth had tied it around her neck. It didn't have a clasp. Where could it have gone? She couldn't have lost it, could she?

Rinsing the shampoo out of her hair, she thought about the dream. She remembered the feeling of Ariana's hands about her throat and the feeling of a noose tightening around her neck. She had a moment of terror as the memory wrapped about her. Then she heard the sound of laughter. Not the musical, lilting notes she had heard when she had first come to this house, but a deep, menacing laugh of triumph. Shaking herself, she listened harder, but only heard the shower pounding against the porcelain tub. She told herself to get in control and to stop letting her imagination run away with her.

Turning off the shower plunged the bathroom into silence except for the tiny dribble of the final remains of water in the pipes. Then she thought she heard the laughter again, only fainter and further away. Old pipes, she thought. Old houses and old pipes.

She dried herself off and wrapped the towel around her hair. Grabbing her robe, she snuggled herself in its warmth. Despite the restorative shower, she still felt drained. Using a towel, she wiped the steam from the mirror and stared at her reflection, slightly warped from the remaining moisture. Her face looked hollow, with dark circles bruising the skin under her eyes. She opened the bathroom door and started down the hall.

"Meow." Reagan stopped in her tracks. "Meow," came the plaintive cry of a cat. I didn't know Willow had a cat, Reagan thought to herself. "Meow." She listened, trying to track where the sound was coming from. "Meow."

"Woof." Now she could hear Wiley barking, but it sounded like he was outside.

She walked to her room, towel drying her hair on the way. Tossing the towel at the foot of her bed, she grabbed her brush and gently worked it through her wet hair as she absently walked to the window. "Woof." Wiley barked again. She looked out the window and saw the dog looking up at her. His tail wasn't wagging. In fact, it was held straight out and stiff. She squinted and looked at him closer. It looked like his hackles were up. "Woof, woof." He barked again, looking at her and bouncing stiff-legged on his front paws.

"Meow." There it was again.

"Woof." Wiley dug at the ground frantically, stared at her and barking. He ran in circles.

"Meow." Wiley must be worried about the cat. Reagan mused.

It must be trapped somewhere, but where? Listening carefully, she absently placed her brush on the dresser and tried to follow the sound of the cat's cries. "Meow." It sounded like it was coming from above her. "Meow." Yes, it was coming from above, from the fourth floor. Reagan moved to the door of her room, following the sound. Wiley was barking frantically. Poor Wiley, she thought, he sounds really worried.

As she walked into the hall, she heard a loud crash behind her. Her brush was lying on the floor near the window. She stared at it in disbelief. How did it get all the way across the room? She had just set it down on the dresser.

"Meow" came the cry again. Reagan moved toward the last flight of stairs that led to the upper floor. "Meeeeooooowww." The cry of the cat sounded so pitiful. The poor thing must have gotten stuck up there somehow. Reagan mounted the stairs, rising closer to the door that shut off the upper floor of the house. "Yowl, meow." The cat's cries grew more insistent, and in the background, Reagan could hear Wiley going crazy outside.

She reached her hand toward the knob of the closed door. She started to turn it when the memory of her aunt telling her she was never to go on the fourth floor flooded her mind. It was as if a soft whisper warned her of her promise. I'm not going on the fourth floor, she told herself. I am just letting this poor, trapped beast out. With that she turned the knob and cracked the door open a foot. Wiley let out a loud, mournful howl as a huge black cat with a jagged white slash of fur on its side streaked from the other side of the door. It stopped, sat down on its haunches, stared up at Reagan and blinked. A cold chill shot through Reagan's body as if she had been hit by lightning. The cat yawned and licked its front paw while holding Reagan's gaze with its own yellow eyes. Reagan felt a trickle of cold sweat bead up along her spine. The cat opened its mouth in a hideous grin. Reagan was powerless to move, mesmerized by the cat's stare. Reagan heard frantic toe nails on hardwood as Wiley came bounding up the stairs. The cat stood, arched its back and spat at Reagan just as Wiley reached the landing. The cat hissed at her one last time and ran hell-bent down the stairs. Wiley skidded on the landing, crashed sideways into the steps, turned and chased the cat back down the stairs.

"You're welcome," Reagan called after the disappearing feline. She turned back to the door, pushing it closed and was surprised at the fetid, damp, chilly air that poured through the opening. Decisively, she shut the door and went down the stairs to her room to finish getting ready for the day.

After straightening her room and making her bed, Reagan picked up her phone from the charger. She had missed a couple of texts. Olivia wanted to know how her date had gone, and Chase wanted to know if she wanted to come over to see how his mom made soap. She sent a quick text off to Olivia telling her it was wonderful, and she would catch up with her later. Then she sent a text to Chase and told him she would love to come, what time, and where.

She glanced at the time and was shocked it was so late. She never slept that late. She doubted that anyone would still be downstairs at breakfast. She tied her Chuck Taylors and trotted down the steps. She was right, there was no one around, but there were some fresh baked blueberry muffins on the sideboard and a few pieces of crispy bacon. Reagan munched on the bacon as she reached in the fridge to get a glass of milk. Her phone chirped with an incoming text. Chase responded with his address and that she should arrive as soon as possible. Reagan snagged three muffins and put them in a plastic bag, chugged her milk and left a note so her aunt would know where she went. She ran upstairs to get her keys and purse.

When she stepped into her room, she caught sight of her starfish necklace. It seemed like it was suspended in the air above her pillow against the headboard. What the hell? As she got closer, she saw that it was caught up on the carving of the near post of the bed. She reached out and plucked it from where it was caught. That's weird, she thought, I'm sure it wasn't there when I made the bed. Her aunt and Cora Rose would say that Adelaide had put it there. Oh well, who was she to argue? Either way, she was happy to have her necklace back. She settled it around her neck, tying a makeshift knot where the other had come untied. She felt a warmth fill her body as the starfish made contact with her flesh. Somewhere in the bowels of the house, the cat howled.

Reagan punched the address that Chase gave her into her phone, allowing the GPS to take over. She put her car in reverse and started to back out the drive. Willow came out of the barn, Wiley sulking behind her. Her aunt raised her hand in a stop gesture, so Reagan put the car in park and stepped out of the car.

"Hey Willow, I left you a note. I'm heading over to Chase's house. His mom is making some soap today, and I'm going to watch."

"That's fine. Give Emma my regards."

"I assume that's Chase's mom," said Reagan

"Yes, it is. Tell her I will call her in a couple of days to let her know when I'm headed to Baltimore."

"Will do. I'll see you later," Willow waved her hand absently in reply. Reagan heard her aunt addressing the dog as she got into the car and put it in reverse.

"What's gotten in to you today? Why are you all mopey and cranky?" Wiley barely wagged his tail. His ears slid down his head, and he looked miserable. Willow stopped walking and looked intently at the dog. She put her hand under his chin and raised his face, looking in his eyes. Then she looked after Reagan's car as it pulled down the driveway. Willow walked back into the barn with a thoughtful look on her face.

Reagan listened to the turn by turn directions from her cell phone as she headed to Chase's. She was a little apprehensive meeting his mom. She had only met a few of the adults in this strange community, and most of them were definitely odd. She had a feeling that a soap making herbalist would be no different. Fifteen minutes later, she pulled into the driveway of an old stone cottage nestled on the edge of a cranberry bog. A large sable and white collie ambled up to the car, greeting Reagan with a kind, trusting look.

"Griff, let Reagan get out of the car." The dog looked back and wagged his tail at Chase as the young man jumped down from the wide front porch and jogged toward the car. "Hey there, sunshine," said Chase as he reached for Reagan's hand and gave her a casual kiss on the cheek.

"Hey, you," Reagan said shyly. She wasn't used to the easy way Chase had slid into a comfortable relationship with her. She was accustomed to the stupid posturing and coy games the teens back home always seemed to play.

"Are you ready to meet my mom and learn the secrets of soap?"

"Sure," she shut the door, and they started for the house. "Oh, wait, hang on." She ran back to the car and retrieved the blueberry muffins. "My tuition payment." She opened the bag and let Chase inhale the heavenly scent.

"Cora Rose's blueberry muffins? I like you even more now than I did last night." Reagan blushed, and Chase laughed.

"Did I just hear something about Cora Rose's famous muffins?" A slight woman with long golden hair came out of a small shed that was covered with climbing roses and other flowering vines. In front of the shed was a beautiful garden laid out in the shape of a Celtic knot, the crushed seashell path showing the lines of the intricate pattern.

"Mom, this is Reagan, and she comes bearing gifts."

"It's a pleasure, Reagan. I am happy to meet the girl who has forced Willow to converse with another human." She clasped Reagan's hands and smiled, looking into her eyes. Reagan was immediately filled with warmth. Kindness radiated from the woman's deep green eyes and the softly lined face. Emma's eyes dropped to Reagan's neck, and she gasped involuntarily. She recovered quickly with a smile.

"What's wrong, Mom?" asked Chase, and Reagan looked uneasily between the two of them.

"Nothing, I just was noticing the beautiful starfish pendant that Reagan is wearing. I haven't seen that in many, many years. Where did you find it, dear?"

"I didn't find it. Seth gave it to me," said Reagan. Emma's eyes darkened, the green turning even more intense.

"Seth, who is Seth?" asked Chase. Emma's mother shook her head slightly at Chase, but Reagan didn't notice.

"Seth is a guy who I met a couple of times down on the cliffs below Willow's house. He said he lived around the curve of the cliff. I'm surprised you don't know him. I thought everyone knew everybody in a small town like this. How could you have seen it before, Mrs. Renault? Seth said he made it for me."

"Call me Emma. May I?" Emma asked as she reached to take the pendant in her hand. Reagan nodded. Emma gently picked up the pendant, lifting it from the hollow of Reagan's throat. She leaned forward and examined it closely. Closing her fingers around the starfish, she closed her eyes and smiled. She stayed that way for a second, then opened her startling green eyes. She smiled warmly at Reagan and said, "It reminds me of a pendant that I knew of a long time ago. It is a striking resemblance. It is a good pendant, full of positive energy. Wear it in good health." She gently lay the starfish back down onto Reagan's skin. Reagan felt the starfish radiate warmth, and she felt a sense of peace.

"So, are we going to eat the muffins or just stand here in the driveway looking at a piece of jewelry some random guy made for you?" Chase asked. Reagan looked at him, surprised, not thinking of the fact that he might be slightly jealous of the situation. He smiled at her and winked. He didn't seem to be taking it too badly.

Emma turned and led them into the knot garden. They wound along the shell path to the side of the whimsical shed where a delicate table and several chairs sat under a tall, sweeping pine tree. Emma took the cozy off a pot of tea and poured while Reagan put the muffins on three exquisite china plates.

"These plates are beautiful, and they look old," said Reagan, "I'm afraid to use them, especially outdoors."

"Yes, they are very old. They were my great-great grandmother's. She would have loved that we are using them outdoors. What is the point of hiding beauty behind glass? Things are much more beautiful when they are in the sunlight and are loved daily. Don't you think? Besides, it is better to be broken, scarred, and loved than it is to be perfect, whole, unloved and alone." Reagan thought about it for a moment and realized that Emma was absolutely right.

They finished the tea and muffins, and Emma asked Chase to go into the house to get the goat's milk from the freezer.

"Goat's milk?" asked Reagan.

"That's the kind of soap I make. I use goat's milk. You will have to meet Hyssop and Lavender. They are my current nannies that I keep for the milk."

"Wait, you have your own goats?"

"Yes, you can meet them later. Once we make the soap, I will take you out to the goat barn." With that Chase walked up holding two large bags of frozen goat milk. "Let's get started," Emma said, as she opened the picturesque shed.

A couple of hours later, they emerged from the shed, Reagan's head swirling with the different fragrance possibilities. She had only been curious when she'd come to see the process of soap making, but now she was hooked. They'd made a new batch by mixing sweet honeysuckle fragrance with a touch of tangerine. The results were heavenly. Emma was trying to come up with a name for their new product along with a sketch for the label but hadn't come up with any good ideas yet. Chase took Reagan to meet the nannies while Emma completed the record keeping. She recorded every step and every weight measurement of each ingredient so she could duplicate the recipe and make another identical batch if the results were favorable.

Reagan was delighted with the goats. The nannies came trotting up to the fence when Chase and Reagan approached. Chase showed Reagan how the goats would nibble her fingers looking for a treat, but these goats were polite and wouldn't bite.

"It's not fair. We don't have a treat for them," said Reagan. Emma came up behind them and handed Chase an apple. He twisted the apple, breaking it in half. He broke the halves in pieces and handed one to Reagan.

"Here you go. They love apples." They fed the goats the apples, and Reagan scratched each one behind the ears. Griff the collie came up and stretched his nose up to Reagan, demanding the same treatment. She laughed and petted the dog.

"They like you," said Emma, as she watched the dog lean against Reagan's legs.

"I like them. I've never had a pet, but now I wish I did. I love Wiley. He is the best dog, and this morning I ran into Willow's cat. I don't know its name, but I don't think he likes me very much."

"Hmmm, I didn't know Willow had a cat. It's not like her. Don't worry about a cat not liking you. It's not in their nature to like people. They merely tolerate them to get the human to do their bidding. Dogs were put here to be companions to people. Cats were put here to torment people. Some cultures thought cats were sent to earth from the devil while other cultures worship the cat. I have to be honest, I've never really met a cat I liked or trusted," said Emma.

"Well, I have nothing to base it on, but I'm not sold on the cat. I do know that when I get to go back home, I am going to ask my mom if I can have a dog."

"What kind of dog do you want?" asked Chase.

"I never really thought about it. I like Wiley a lot, but Griff is beautiful. This is a collie, right?"

"Yes. He is a sable and white rough collie. I'm not surprised that you like him. Your father had a collie when he was young. His collie came from the same breeder as this one."

"That's right. I heard that story from Willow. The dog died trying to save my dad."

"Your dad loved that dog."

"Wait, this dog is from that guy, I forget his name, that my dad had to save a bunch of money for and then walked a long way to get the dog?"

Yes, this dog is a Whitstock dog. The line is very old. Whitstock has been breeding collies for as long as anyone can remember, and the man is as old as dirt," said Emma.

"It would be so cool to have a Whitstock collie, just like my dad. They are really expensive, though, aren't they?"

"Yes, they do cost a pretty penny, although occasionally, a pup is born that isn't quite up to Whitstock's standards. A lot of breeders would destroy the dog, but Whitstock's never done that. He makes sure the animal can't be bred, and then he finds the offensive pup a good home. Griff here was one of those offensive puppies."

"What's wrong with Griff? He's beautiful," cried Reagan.

"His right ear doesn't tip just right, and his tail has a crooked spot," laughed Chase. "He just isn't a pretty collie, are you buddy? You old, ugly cur."

"I think he is absolutely perfect. I wonder if Mr. Whitstock has any offensive puppies that I could buy. I wonder if my mom would let me have one?"

"Well, I have to deliver some of my calendula salve to him. One of his dogs got cut up on some barbed wire. He likes to use my herbal salve because it is natural. I was going to take it to him tomorrow. Would you like to come along?"

"I would love to. As long as I'm not intruding."

"Not at all, my dear. I look forward to it. Now would you two like to throw some hamburgers on the grill for lunch while I make up a salad?"

"Sure, Mom. You go pick some salad and I'll fire up the grill."

"Pick some salad?" asked Reagan.

"Yeah, Mom has a kitchen garden at the side of the house. Anytime we want a salad, she just goes to the kitchen garden and picks everything fresh. Why don't you go with her while I grab some burgers and get the grill going?"

Reagan followed Emma around to the back of the cottage. There was a white picket fence surrounding a neat garden with rows of different types of lettuce, spinach, carrots, and other vegetables. Emma handed her a basket and showed her which lettuce leaves were ready to harvest and how to know which carrot was plump enough to pull. When the basket was full, Emma took it into the house.

"You'll find Chase on the side of the house at the grill. I can already smell the burgers cooking. I'll wash the greens and bring the salad out in a few minutes."

"Can I help you with anything else?" asked Reagan.

"No, but thank you. My guess is Chase is sulking because you aren't out there with him. I will join you two in a minute."

Reagan rounded the corner of the house to find a stone patio with a large wooden table flanked with mismatched wooden chairs. Chase flourished a grill spatula as he expertly flipped a burger.

"Rare as in your beauty, or well-done as in your kindness, my lady?" Reagan made pantomimed gagging, then laughed.

"How about medium like the average person I really am."

"You are anything but average, Reagan. I just don't think you know it yet." He reached for her hand and pulled her close to him.

Her heart beat faster in her chest as she looked up into his eyes. He lowered his face and gently brushed his lips against hers. She responded, pressing closer to him. He groaned and playfully bit her lower lip, tugging gently. She opened her eyes and saw he was watching her, amused.

"Your mother is going to see us," Reagan said, nervously.

"My dear, my mother doesn't have to see us to know exactly what is going on."

"What do you mean?"

"Oh, you will figure out soon enough that my mother knows things. It's just the way it is. She just knows things."

CHAPTER 18

*R*eagan sat on the porch absently petting Wiley. He sat on her feet and leaned heavily against her legs. He was tense and obviously unhappy.

"What's the matter, boy? Why are you acting the way you are?" asked Reagan. He looked up at her, his eyes deep pools of sadness. "Do you miss Willow? She should be home tomorrow." Wiley thumped his tail, but only one wag. He leaned harder against her tilting his head back so she could scratch his throat. He cried softly and looked out into the evening fog rising over the cliff. He was clearly one unhappy dog.

"Are you sick?" She looked at the dog, now getting worried. "Maybe you ate something that made you sick. I'm not sure what to do." She remembered something about dog's noses needing to be cold and wet. She reached around and touched the end of the dog's snout. It was cold and damp. That was good, right? Looking at him closely, she decided something just wasn't right. She pulled out her phone and texted Chase, telling him that Wiley was acting weird. She waited for a text back. Instead, the phone rang. The caller id let her know it was Chase.

"Hey Chase, I'm sorry for bothering you, but I'm really worried about Wiley."

"Reagan, it's Emma. What's going on?"

"He looks sad and mopey. He keeps leaning on me like he wants something, and he keeps whimpering."

"Is he throwing up or does he have diarrhea? Will he eat food?"

"I don't think he has thrown up or anything. Let me go get one of your puppy biscuits." She went into the kitchen and reached into the glass apothecary jar where Emma's homemade puppy biscuits were kept for Wiley. He followed her, sticking to her leg like glue. When she offered the biscuit, he took it, holding it in his mouth as he followed her back out to the porch. He laid down and half-heartedly ate the biscuit, watching her with sad eyes the whole time.

"He ate the biscuit, but he just seems unhappy."

"Since he ate, I wouldn't be too worried. He probably misses Willow. Also, it sounds like he really feels the need to protect you, so let him stay with you when he wants to. Can you do that? Do you want me to come over and check him?"

"No, I think we'll be fine. He just left me and is whimpering at the kitchen door."

"Does he have to go out?"

"No, he wants in. We are sitting on the porch right now."

"It's getting dark. He won't want to be out in the dark, and he will want you in, so why don't you lock up for the night? If you're worried or nervous, just call or text Chase and we will head over. Okay? Oh, and Reagan, keep that starfish necklace on. It has good mojo. Good night, sweetie."

Reagan reached up and rubbed the necklace. As always, the smooth metal was slightly warm to the touch. Yeah, everyone in this town is completely nuts, but she really didn't mind when it was Emma talking nuts. In fact, it actually felt comforting.

She took the dog in the house and locked the doors. She left the little sconce light on in the kitchen. Grabbing a glass of water, she looked down at Wiley. "Come on buddy. Let's go to bed." Wiley followed right beside Reagan. When they crossed through the dining room, Wiley whimpered, shivering. He whipped his head back and forth like he was looking for something. As Reagan left the dining room, entering the great hall to mount the stairs, she heard a snarling and snapping behind her. Turning her head, she saw the glowing eyes and the outline of wolves crouched under the dining room table. They took a menacing step forward.

Reagan ran up the stairs and slammed the bedroom door behind her as Wiley tucked his tail between his legs and edged his way into the room just in time. Her heart was pounding, a cold sweat breaking out on her neck, and her hands were shaking wildly. All the time she had been denying something strange was happening, but now, reality was staring her in the face. For the first time, Reagan noticed a small ornate turnkey above the engraved door knob. She hesitated and then turned it. She heard a smooth click. Turning the doorknob, she tried to open the door, but it held fast. The ornate turnkey was a deadbolt, designed to keep people out. Right now, she wanted to keep things out, but would a dead bolt work against things that weren't real? Would it work against the wolves with the red eyes and slashing teeth?

Wiley whimpered and leaned against her. He looked up at Reagan and whined. She scratched his ears and looked around the room. She'd always felt safe and comforted here in this room. Now, she was uneasy, like something was out of place. She glanced at her dresser. Everything was neatly where she left it. The rocking chair was still, and her library books were next to her bed. That's what she needed. She needed to crawl into bed and read, snuggled under the covers with Wiley curled up beside her.

Reagan pulled on her pajamas, the soft pair of shorts and an oversized tee shirt that said, Ohio University. She was feeling calmer, but she realized that she hadn't brushed her teeth. No way was she leaving her room tonight. It would have to wait. She plugged in her cell phone and crawled in bed. She motioned for

Wiley to jump up and join her, but Wiley hesitated. He whined softly again. His worried look made Reagan feel nervous all over again. She patted the bed beside her a second time. Wiley sighed and jumped up, settling tightly against her.

Reagan opened her book and sank against the headboard when her cellphone alerted her that a text had come through. It was Chase asking her if she was awake. She replied that she was. The phone rang in her hand, startling her.

"Hey," said Reagan.

"Hey, yourself. Are you okay? Mom said you sounded nervous. Are you just worried about Wiley, or is there something else?"

"No, everything is fine…" said Reagan, hesitantly.

"Reagan," said Chase, softly, "what's going on? I know something is wrong. I can feel it."

"It's just, I can't believe I'm saying this, but maybe I'm losing my mind or something…"

"Honey, just tell me. You can trust me. I won't think you're crazy or anything. What happened tonight?"

"I saw the wolves," Reagan whispered and waited, her heart beating hard against her chest. "I saw the wolves, and I heard them snarling and snapping their jaws." She waited for his response, but it was quiet on the other end. Her heart sank, and she felt silly and small, like a frightened child on Halloween.

"I believe you."

Chase's words came through the phone strong and clear. Reagan let go of the breath she didn't realize she was holding. He said it again,

"Honey, I believe you, and I'm coming over."

"No, you don't have to do that. I'm okay. I've got Wiley with me and I… I, um, locked myself in my bedroom, so I am really okay."

"I don't like the thought of you being scared and alone, and I know you are feeling that way," said Chase. Reagan smiled to herself and felt a bit better. Chase believed her, as crazy as it all sounded, he believed her. She felt braver, too. She knew she could get through the night okay.

"Really, I'm okay now. I don't understand what I saw, or what it means, but I am okay. I'm tired, and I'm going to go to sleep now. I will talk to you in the morning."

"Okay if you're sure. Wait, hang on." Reagan could hear murmuring in the background. "Mom says you'll be fine. Keep your starfish necklace on your neck and Wiley beside you. Those things will make you feel safe and protected. I will call you in the morning. If you need anything, if you're scared or need to talk, just call. Don't worry about waking me up, and if you need me, I will be there in a heartbeat. I promise."

"Thanks, Chase, but I'll be just fine. Good night." Reagan clicked off the phone call and put her book up on the nightstand. She studied the room one last time, satisfied that everything was okay, and she clicked the light off.

Darkness filled the room, and Wiley whined softly. He pressed his cold nose against Reagan's cheek and licked her with just the tip of his tongue. In just a few minutes, Reagan's eyes had adjusted to the dark. She waited tensely, listening for any noises that seemed out of place. It was quiet. Soon, despite her nerves, Reagan fell into a restless sleep, Wiley watchful beside her.

CHAPTER 19

*R*eagan was lying in a deep hole in the ground. It was cold and damp. She tried to move, but she couldn't. High above her, someone stood, a woman in a long dress. She was holding a shovel. The woman looked in the hole and smiled a wicked, haunting smile. Her eyes were wild, and her dark hair was blowing behind her in the wind. She laughed defiantly and dug up a shovelful of dirt. Then with a gleeful laugh, she tossed the shovel of dirt into the hole. It landed on Reagan's chest, pelting her with small rocks. Dirt bounced off, peppering her face, particles sticking to her lips and landing in her eyes.

Another shovelful came down, followed by two more. The weight of the dirt was pressing down on her chest. She struggled wildly, trying to get up, but it was hopeless. Even her eyelids wouldn't listen to her commands as they stared wide open at the crazy lady above her throwing shovelful after shovelful of dirt on top of her. The weight was becoming oppressive, and it was getting harder and harder to breathe. Her lips were getting covered, and dirt was filling up her nose.

Two shovelfuls landed on her neck, pressing down on her larynx. Soon she would suffocate or be crushed to death. The hysteria in her mind was building as she tried to decide which would come first and which would be worse. Another shovelful, this one landing directly on her face, covered her mouth completely and her left nostril and eye, the lids still wide open. She tried to scream through dirt piled on her lips, but nothing would come out, and she couldn't draw enough of a breath to try to scream again. Her right eye was still focused on the woman above her. Their eyes locked, and the lady screamed as she threw the last shovelful down on Reagan's face.

"I TOLD YOU TO GO AWAY. I TOLD YOU TO STAY AWAY FROM SETH!" The pile of dirt landed with a thud on Reagan's right eye and fell down into her right nostril, cutting off her breath completely.

Reagan gasped and struggled against the weight on her chest. She fought against the pressure on her throat as her eyes flew open. Moonlight bathed her room, and she found herself staring into the eyes of a cat. It blinked mildly at her and pressed its weight down harder, its front paws pushing down on Reagan's larynx. She froze in fear, locked in a stare with the animal.

The cat slowly extended its front claws while holding Reagan's eyes with its gaze. The claws pierced her throat drawing beads of blood. Reagan gasped, breaking the spell, now fully awake. Wiley leapt up snapping and growling, chasing the cat from the bed. The cat ran to the door, yowling wildly, Wiley hot on its heels. With its back to the door, the cat spun around and faced Wiley fearlessly. It arched its back and spat a warning, then lashed out with its claws, catching Wiley's soft nose. Wiley yelped in pain. Reagan jumped out of bed, running for the door. She flipped the turnkey lock, careful to stay away from the slashing claws, and opened the door. The cat flew out of the room with a malevolent glance back over its shoulder. Wiley chased it into the hallway, then turned and came back to press his weight against Reagan's thighs.

"Are you okay, buddy?" Reagan asked as she peered down at Wiley's bloodied nose. "Come on, let's fix that."

She led the dog to the bathroom and gently cleaned off his nose. Luckily, the scratches were superficial, so she didn't think he would need medical attention. "Let's go back to bed. You can snuggle with me, but you need to do a better job keeping away my bad dreams." She shook her head, trying to recall what she had been dreaming right before she woke up. Something about a woman and being buried alive. The woman said something to her, something that was important, but she couldn't remember what it was.

She and Wiley got back to her bedroom. She closed the door again and turned the lock. She was feeling a little silly about it, but she felt better with the door locked. When she crawled back in bed, she noticed her phone was vibrating. Chase was calling her.

"Hello?"

"Reagan, are you okay? What happened?"

"I just had a bad dream, that's all, and I woke up with the stupid cat sitting on my chest... wait, how did you know something was wrong?"

"I woke up and had a feeling... that's all. Are you sure you're all right?"

"I'm fine. Just a bad dream." Reagan absently fingered her throat where the cat's claws had pierced the skin. "That's weird," she said.

"What's weird?"

"My starfish necklace. It's not there. That's the second time it's come off at night. I wonder where it is."

"What, it's not on your neck?"

"No, it was there when I went to sleep. It must be somewhere in the sheets, but I can't find it. I will look for it in the morning. Go to sleep, Chase. I'm okay. I'll call you tomorrow."

"If you're sure. Call me when you get up, please." Reagan smiled to herself. She kind of liked the protective side of Chase.

"I will. As soon as I wake up, I will give you a call. Goodnight, again." She put her phone down and turned on her side, spooning Wiley and closed her eyes to go to sleep.

Outside her bedroom door, the black cat with the white slash of fur on its side stalked back and forth staring at the door and growling a low growl. On the bed, Wiley kept his eyes glued on the light seeping from under the door. He watched the shadow of the cat's legs as it paced. The dog sighed and settled in for a long night. He refused to fall asleep again.

CHAPTER 20

*R*eagan woke to her phone vibrating incessantly on the bedside table. Wiley sighed and whined. He stretched his back in an arc while still laying curled against Reagan. He licked her chin, stood in the bed, and stretched again. He looked over at her vibrating phone and whined.

Reagan reached out a stiff arm and picked up the phone. Her skin tingled as the blood flowed into the still sleeping arm.

"Hello," Reagan croaked. She cleared her throat, trying again. "Hello?"

"Hey. Good morning." It was Chase. "Did you survive the night? Is Wiley okay?"

"Yeah. He seems like he is fine. He spent the night with me on my bed. He looks tired, but I think he is okay."

"He is tired because he watched over you the whole night."

"How do you know that?" asked Reagan, looking at the dog, curiously.

"Because I know dogs, and I know Wiley. His job is to make sure the people he loves are safe."

"Well, I am safe. That was such a weird night. I had such horrible dreams."

"Did you have any more after I talked to you?"

"I think so. I just remember feeling scared, like someone or something was constantly watching me. Of course, Wiley probably was, so that isn't so far off, huh?"

"What are you going to do today?"

"I don't have a clue. I am so out of sorts. I think I'll take a walk down to the ocean. I haven't been down there for a while. The fresh sea air will probably clear my head."

"Hey, why don't I come over and go down there with you?"

"Sure, if you want, but you don't need to babysit me. I'm okay, you know. My imagination just ran away with me last night."

"Did you ever find your starfish necklace?"

"I haven't looked yet. When I get up and make the bed, I'll check in the sheets. I'm sure it's here somewhere. The string probably came untied. I'm going to go take a shower and get something to eat. I can smell bacon cooking, and Cora Rose doesn't like to be kept waiting."

"No kidding. Maybe I can score a muffin or something when I stop by."

"Sounds like a plan. I'll see you in a bit."

Reagan stretched lazily and then got out of bed. She looked all through the sheets trying to find her necklace, but it was nowhere to be seen. She smoothed the sheets and bedspread, setting the pillows up against the headboard. She got on her hands and knees and looked under the bed, but there was nothing there. That's odd, she thought. It couldn't have walked off by itself. She grabbed her robe, looking one last time on the floor for the necklace, then left the room for her shower.

Freshly showered and dressed, Reagan headed downstairs for breakfast. Wiley must have gone down while she was in the shower because there was no sign of him. As she stepped off the bottom step and turned toward the great hall and the dining room. Reagan hesitated. She looked at the huge table, her heart pounding in fear. Remembering last night, and the snarling and snapping of teeth, Reagan peered under the table from the safe distance of the hall. There were no signs of the wolves. Damn, she was losing it, she told herself. Straightening her shoulders, she walked briskly into the dining room and marched past the table. As she cleared the final corner, she heard the snap of teeth. She jumped and scurried to the kitchen, refusing to look back. Cora Rose looked up from the stove where she was removing a waffle from the iron.

"You look as pale as a ghost. Are you sick, girl?" asked Cora Rose, holding the spatula in the air. "You have a fever or something?"

Reagan shook her head.

"I'm fine, I just didn't sleep well. When did you get back, Aunt Willow?"

"About an hour ago. Couldn't miss a Cora Rose breakfast," said Willow.

Reagan grabbed a plate from the sideboard and loaded it with bacon and waffles. Willow glanced up from her breakfast, holding a Pepsi in one hand and watched Reagan. Her eyes narrowed as she studied her.

Suddenly, a chill descended upon the kitchen, frigid air seemed to swirl around Reagan. Willow stared hard at Reagan and cautiously asked her, "Did you by any chance go up to the fourth floor?"

Cora Rose stiffened at the stove.

"No, of course not. I've never been up there. Why?"

"No reason, I was just curious."

"Nope, I have respected your wishes. Although I must say I've been curious and wanted to explore, but I ignored those urges." Reagan munched on her waffles thoughtfully. "Oh, yeah, I did let the cat out, though."

Cora gasped, and the large metal spoon clattered to the cooktop.

"You what?" asked Willow, holding Reagan's eyes in a steely glare.

"Your cat must have gotten trapped up there somehow. I let it out. It was yowling at the door. I opened the door and the poor thing ran hell-bent for the stairs. I didn't know you had a cat. This whole time I've been living here, I've never seen it."

"May the good Lord have mercy on our souls," muttered Cora Rose as she took off her apron and walked out the kitchen door.

Reagan ran for the cliff path, tears streaming down her face. Willow's harsh words rang in her ears.

"I don't know why I ever agreed to let you stay here. I only asked one thing of you, that you not go on the fourth floor, and you disregarded my wishes. Now, we are all going to pay the consequences of your actions."

Reagan explained again that she didn't go up to the fourth floor, but she had just opened the door to let the trapped animal free. She didn't understand what she did wrong. All she knew was Cora Rose wasn't coming back, and Willow didn't want her at the house any longer. Her mom was halfway across the world, and she was so very alone.

The wind was picking up, tearing at her hair as she turned at the top of the cliff and headed down the trail to the beach. She was temporarily blinded by her tears, and she tripped over a rock, falling to her knees. She slammed the palms of her hands into the ground in her attempt to break her fall. Scrambling to her feet, she wiped her eyes with her dirty, bloody hands and ran even faster down the path. Her knees screamed out in pain, but she didn't bother to stop to pull the embedded stones from her flesh.

She wanted to run and put the house, Cora Rose, and her aunt behind her.

She hit the rocks at the bottom of the cliff at an all-out run. She didn't realize that the tide was coming in and the ocean was swirling dangerously close to the cliff base. She flung herself down on her favorite flat rock, buried her head in the crook of her elbow and allowed herself to sob uncontrollably. All the pain and frustration of the summer was just too overwhelming. The things she didn't understand and couldn't explain weren't helping the situation. She felt like she was losing her mind, slowly but steadily, and she felt a gnawing icy spot of fear in her gut. Normally she wasn't the kind of person to be afraid. She was used to being self-confident and meeting the world head on, but this whole summer was beginning to erode that confidence. And now, she had royally screwed up, but she didn't even know how it had happened.

Her body shuddered again, and she let herself cry it out. A gull screamed above her. Instinctively, she reached for the necklace, forgetting that the starfish was no longer around her neck. Of course, this made her cry even harder. She heard the flap of wings just over her head. Great, she was going to be attacked by a damn bird again. Covering the back of her head with her hands she rolled into a tight ball, waiting the onslaught of talons. She didn't have the energy to get up and run. A wing hit her ear, followed by the peck of a beak. She cried out in pain and swatted at the gull. Another bird tore at the flesh of her arms, a third ripped a chunk from her neck. She thrashed at the birds, striking one of them, but they renewed their efforts, beating her with their wings.

She felt a strong hand at her back. Peeking out from under her arm, she saw that Seth had crouched above her and was swatting at the birds. Now there were even more of them. A small flock of birds was wheeling in the sky. Mixed with the scream of gulls was the same maniacal laughter Reagan had heard in her dream.

"Where is your necklace?" asked Seth, "Where is the starfish I made you?" He sounded angry and demanding. Reagan hiccupped as she answered.

"It was on my neck last night when I went to sleep. Then sometime in the night, I had a horrible dream. It was awful, and I was dying." Suddenly, the dream came back to her in vivid detail. "Ariana was trying to kill me by burying me alive. When I woke up, the cat was sitting on my chest, and his claws were pressing into my throat. After that, I couldn't find my necklace." Reagan sobbed again, and another bird hit the top of her head, slashing with its beak.

"Ariana?" whispered Seth. "Ariana is back? How was she set free?" But now he was yelling, his voice filled with rage.

"She was just in my dream. How could she be set free? She lived a long, long time ago. What the hell is wrong with all you people?" Reagan stood up defiantly, facing Seth. Her tear stained face was now no longer afraid but furious and ready to fight. She was ready to give him a piece of her mind when a large black gull flew right into her face and tore at her hair with its sharp talons, its cry sounding more like a laugh than ever.

"Hey," a voice shouted from the path. "Hey, get away from her." Chase came running, Wiley sprinting ahead, barking and snapping in anger. Wiley reached Reagan first, leaping into the air, trying to bite the gulls. Chase pulled his hoodie off, wrapped it around Reagan's bloodied head and pulled her sobbing into his chest.

His arms wrapped tightly, protectively around her as he watched the gulls retreat out to sea. Wiley whined and licked Reagan's hands, struggling to get close to her, but she was snuggled deep into Chase's chest, his sweatshirt and arms guarding her from danger. Reagan turned her head to look at Seth, but he had vanished. She stared in disbelief. She whipped her head wildly around looking for any sign of Seth, then she looked up into Chase's face, and her eyes went vacant.

Reagan collapsed against him, and he swept her into his arms, carrying her like she was a feather. He carried her all the way up the cliff, never faltering as Reagan cried softly against his shirt. He gently placed her in the passenger seat of his car and closed the door. Wiley whimpered and barked incessantly, so Chase opened the back door, letting the dog jump in. Wiley leaned over the back of the front seat gently licking Reagan, trying to calm her. Chase got in the driver's seat and drug Reagan close to him. Keeping his right arm tightly around her shoulders, he reached awkwardly over the steering wheel, started his car and backed out of the driveway. Willow watched the proceedings from the front porch. As he drove away, Chase locked eyes with Willow. She nodded then turned to go into the house.

CHAPTER 21

*E*mma met Chase's car as it pulled into the driveway. She reached into the car and wrapped a soft, woolen throw around Reagan's shoulders. Griff whined softly, pushing his nose into the car to see what he could do. Chase came around to the passenger side and gently scooted Reagan across the seat and out of the car. Realizing she wasn't going to stand, he lifted her effortlessly and followed his mom into the cottage.

Chase sniffed the air as they entered the cozy house.

"Jasmine," said Emma. "It will help to calm her. Just hold her and let the herb work its magic."

The burning incense scented the cottage as Chase sank on an overstuffed couch near the fireplace, Reagan still curled up in his lap. Both Wiley and Griff settled companionably at his feet. Reagan's sobbing had turned to quiet weeping in the car, and now she was frighteningly still, her eyes open in a vacant stare.

"Mom?" said Chase, his voice filled with worry.

"Just give her time. She is in shock, terrified and confused."

"Mom, she didn't grow up here. She doesn't understand things the way we do. I don't know if she is going to be okay."

"Trust me. She is going to be fine."

The old-fashioned phone on the kitchen wall rang. Emma crossed the room to answer. Chase pulled Reagan closer to him, rocking her gently against him. He heard the murmur of his mom's voice.

"Yes, she's here. Chase has her. I'm burning some Jasmine and brewing peppermint tea. We will keep her here as long as she needs to stay… Yes, I can do that. Either Chase or I will purify the house with some sage, and I will bring rosemary. Do you think that's wise, Willow? I know you have a business to run but going out of town right now might not be a good idea. Yes, we will watch out for Reagan. Okay. Let me know if you need anything, and Willow, please be careful."

"She's leaving? Just like that. This happens, and she is going to take off? Don't you think she has a little responsibility here? Typical Willow, just pretending nothing is wrong," Chase voiced with disgust. Reagan whimpered in his arms.

"Shhhh. Now is not the time. Lower your voice," Emma warned. She crouched down in front of the couch holding a cup of fragrant peppermint tea.

"Reagan? Reagan, honey, I want you to sit up and try to drink this. I promise it will make you feel better." Emma placed a hand gently on Reagan's arm, offering the tea with the other hand. Reagan moved deeper into Chase's chest. "Reagan, I understand you are scared and confused, but I really want you to drink this." Emma looked at Chase. "You try. See if you can get her to have a sip."

She set the cup and saucer down on the old chest in front of the couch. Then she carefully backed away. Griff stood up and placed a paw on Reagan's hip. He nudged her with his long pencil-shaped nose. Chase placed his hand under Reagan's chin and carefully lifted her face until he could look into her unseeing eyes.

"Reagan, honey, please." He reached down and softly kissed her forehead. "For me, sweetheart? Please come back to me." Wiley whined from the floor. Emma smiled, knowing the magic that the dogs and her son could work. Reagan would respond to the love and caring that was surrounding her. Griff started to wag his tail. He licked Reagan's arm. Wiley stood up, whimpered and licked her, too. Both dogs sensed a changed was coming. Following their lead, Chase tried again.

"Reagan, the tea is ready. How 'bout you drink a couple of sips? Come on, sit up a little." Chase shifted her into a sitting position, still keeping her snuggled up against his side. He looked carefully in her face. Her eyes were beginning to lose the lost stare. She closed them and sighed. He felt her trembling against him. As if on cue, his mom brought another blanket and tucked it around Reagan.

"Thank you," Reagan whispered. "Thank you." A large tear rolled silently down her cheek. Chase reached up with his thumb and gently swiped it away. He lifted the cup to her lips, and she took a tentative sip. The warm peppermint tea flooded her with instant comfort. She took another restorative drink. Emma and Chase looked at each other. Reagan was going to be fine. Now comes the hard part, Chase thought, somehow we have to explain this to her. Across the room, Emma nodded, agreeing with Chase's unvoiced concern.

"I DON'T UNDERSTAND any of it. Nothing makes sense to me," Reagan said, quietly. "Ever since I came here I feel like I've been losing my mind."

"You're not losing your mind," Chase said, firmly.

"Okay, I hear what you're saying, but I think you are just trying to be nice and protective. You just want me to feel better," protested Reagan.

"Chase wants you to feel better, but that's not why he's saying it. He's saying it because there is nothing wrong with your mind, other than that it is trying to protect you from yourself. Your mind doesn't want you to deal with things that are hard for you to understand, so it wants to shut down. You aren't like that. You like to deal with things head on, so that's what we are going to do. Are you ready to do that?" asked Emma.

"I think so, but could I please have another cup of tea?"

By the time Emma came back with the second cup of tea, Reagan was settled back on the couch. Chase clasped her left hand loosely.

"I brought some ginger cookies, too. They will help settle your stomach." Reagan looked up startled.

"How did you know my stomach was upset?"

"Well, it doesn't take a mind reader to realize a person's stomach would be upset after having a scare and crying for a good hour. That's enough to send anyone's system into spasms, but it is time to be honest with each other. The thing is, Reagan, you have to be willing to accept what we say. Are you ready to try to do that?" Emma's eyes searched Reagan's. Reagan nodded hesitantly.

"Okay," said Emma, "First of all, I have a gift. Actually, Chase has it, too, but his isn't developed yet. We have the ability to perceive things. It doesn't work all the time, but often we recognize when something is going to happen, a premonition of things to come. More often, we are just really in tune with other people's thoughts and feelings. It's an uncomfortable gift, because we find out things we don't always want to know."

"You know how you said everyone wondered why I didn't date?" asked Chase. Reagan nodded. "Well, it's because I knew what people were thinking. The girls who liked me? I knew what was in their hearts, and I wasn't exactly happy with the kind of people they were. Olivia, she's nice, but her heart is set on someone else. Darcy, well that's a whole other story." Reagan smiled at that, then looked up at Chase.

"But you went out with me."

"Yep, you are a kind and strong person. I like that. You don't have mean thoughts."

"But I do. I think everyone in this town is nuts... or at least I did. I was a horrible, judgmental person."

"Not at all. You didn't understand why people thought the way they did, but you weren't mean about it. You stood up for yourself. You weren't a victim, but you were never intentionally cruel to anyone." Reagan blushed when she thought of how she acted that day to Cora Rose when she accused Cora of moving her brush and other things.

In unison, Chase and Emma said, "Well, no one's perfect." That broke the tension and even Reagan laughed a little.

"So, you know everything that has happened to me? Why didn't you say something before?"

"It's not like watching TV. We don't see everything in your life. Usually, it's like picking up on an emotion, or a feeling. Chase felt you were scared the other night, so he called you. It ended up you were having a bad dream, but he doesn't know what the dream was about. He just knows you were terrified. He knew to go to the cliff today because you were really frightened, and he knew you were hurt. Now that you are more comfortable, I would like to clean you up a bit. The seagulls did a number on you, didn't they?"

Reagan looked down at her arms where the birds had ripped her flesh with their beaks. Her heart twisted with fear. She didn't think she could ever walk near the ocean again. Emma got a warm cloth soaked in an herbal tincture and cleaned Reagan's face and arms. She parted Reagan's long hair and dabbed where the birds had attacked her scalp. Once she was done cleaning, she spread some sweet-smelling ointment on the wounds and bandaged her arms loosely with some soft cotton gauze.

While his mother worked on Reagan, Chase built a small fire in the cottage fireplace. Despite the fact that it was summer, Chase thought a fire would help make Reagan relax and feel comfortable. She smiled at him appreciatively.

Reagan took a deep breath and snuggled back against Chase. The fire crackled merrily, and the dogs slept curled around each other on the hearth. Emma sat in her rocking chair, her knitting in her hands, a cup of tea by her side. Reagan and Chase nibbled on ginger cookies while Reagan told her story. She talked of the brush and how it was moved every night. She mentioned the slippers and the rocking chair moving. All of these things she felt she could explain. She mentioned that Willow thought she might be sleep walking. Emma and Chase listened thoughtfully, nodding occasionally and even smiling sometimes in encouragement.

"But those things were just annoying. The dreams were scary, but they were just dreams, but the wolves..." Emma looked up sharply from her knitting.

"The wolves?"

"I saw the wolves under the table. They came after me, snarling and snapping. They tried to get me."

"When did this happen?" asked Emma.

"Yesterday."

"Was this after you let the cat out?" asked Emma.

"Yeah, but what is the big deal about the damn cat?" shouted Reagan, her voice rising, taking on a hysterical tone.

"Shh, honey, it's okay," soothed Chase. Reagan shrugged his arm off of her impatiently. She was getting angry. Chase smiled.

"Why are you smiling? What the hell is wrong with everybody? AND WHAT ABOUT THE F'ING CAT?"

"I'm smiling because you've got your fight back, and that's good," said Chase as he reached for her again. She allowed herself to be drawn back to the sofa.

"I am going to explain to you about the damn cat," said Emma, "but you have to allow yourself to believe. Can you do that?"

Reagan nodded, slightly, still not sure if she wanted to hear what Emma was about to say.

Emma got up and moved over to the bookcase. She reached up, standing on her tiptoes to reach the top shelf, and she brought down a small ancient looking volume. Reagan was startled when she recognized it. It was Adelaide's diary.

"No, honey, not Adelaide's but Ariana's. You know who that is, right?" Reagan nodded. "You know they were sisters?"

"Yes, but that's really all I know. I started reading Adelaide's journal, but she just kept gushing about this guy with the initial, S." Reagan didn't miss the glance between Chase and Emma.

"The man Adelaide was in love with was a sailor named Seth McCabe." Emma paused, watching Reagan carefully. She saw the moment of understanding in Reagan's eyes.

"Seth? As in my Seth? The Seth that gave me the starfish? And you knew this, but you let me go on about him? You didn't tell me he was... I don't know... not real? What the hell?"

Reagan missed the pain in Chase's eyes when Reagan called him her Seth. Emma looked at her son and smiled, reassuring him not to fret. He relaxed and stroked Reagan's hair soothing her, careful not to touch where the gulls had attacked.

"Yes, the same. Chase didn't tell you because you weren't ready to hear. You weren't ready to believe. Here. Listen to this." Emma carefully opened the old journal and turned the pages, skimming the contents.

"Here it is..." She began reading, *"Adelaide came running up to the porch today. Her hair had slipped its pins and her cheeks were glowing. The sparkle in her eyes nauseates me. I hate her giddy silliness. She is such a child, but she wants to be grown up. She has no idea what it is to be a woman. I tried to ignore her, but she was all excited about some gift. Then she showed me a delicate metal starfish on a knotted cord. It is intriguing, yet for some reason it repulses me. I hate it. She gushed on about how Seth had made it for her. He said it would protect her and remind her of him when he is out to sea. What she doesn't realize is he will only be thinking of me on his next voyage. That silly little twit of a sister has no idea what a man wants or needs. I do, and I will make sure he knows I am the one he misses."*

Reagan's eyes flashed with disgust. "Ariana was a horrible person. She knew Adelaide loved Seth. Why would she write such horrible things?"

"It gets a lot worse. She didn't just write horrible things, but she did horrible things. She visited a woman who lived on the edge of the bog.

"The Widow Hobbs?"

"Exactly. The Widow Hobbs was an herbalist, some would call her a witch. She wasn't a bad person, but she made her living by providing potions and tinctures for the people of the area. Her husband had died, leaving her penniless. She had a child to raise and the only money she could make was by providing her herbal remedies. Some people wanted potions for clearing their skin, or settling their stomach, just like the ginger cookies and the peppermint tea you are drinking. The Widow Hobbs cared for the people who came to her.

Other people had darker needs, an unwanted pregnancy that needed terminated, some rats that needed poisoned. She took care of those needs, too. She even made potions that would guarantee that the person who drank it would fall in love with the person who served it. Ariana came to the widow seeking an attraction potion. She was determined to win Seth. Coupled with the fact she had no problem offering her body as a guarantee Seth would fall for her, Ariana couldn't fail in her plan. At least that is what she thought.

"In the meantime, Seth proposed to Adelaide. After a lot of discussion, Adelaide's father agreed to the marriage. Adelaide was so happy, but Ariana was plotting. She was not going to let this thing happen.

"One night, under the cover of darkness, she led Seth to believe she was Adelaide. Apparently, she had managed to slip the attraction potion in his drink, so he was confused. Ariana took advantage of him. Once he realized what he had done, he cursed her for all time. She just laughed, certain she would get what she wanted. As the wedding day approached, Ariana grew more and more confident and smug. Seth would be hers. Seth was torn up with the guilt of what he had done, but he convinced himself that it was a mistake. It was only once, and it would never happen again. He loved Adelaide, and that's all that mattered. Emma sighed. Griff looked up at his mistress and whimpered.

"On the morning of the wedding day, Ariana gleefully told Seth that she was pregnant, and that he was the father. Devastated and angry, he denied that it could be his, and he said that he would never love her or her demon child. Furious, Ariana threatened to tell Adelaide. He laughed at her and left her. He went to find Adelaide, eager to take his vows with her.

"Adelaide's mother stopped Seth from entering the house, reminding him that a groom must never see the bride before the ceremony on their wedding day. Ariana entered the back of the house and went to meet her sister. Playing the part of the perfect maid of honor, Ariana told Adelaide that Seth wanted to see her. He had a gift for her, and he wanted her to have it before the wedding. He was waiting for her on the cliff by the ocean. Ariana gushed about how romantic it was for her to secretly meet him there before they got married.

"Adelaide rushed to meet her groom. The next thing that anyone knew, they found her body crushed on the rocks below. There was speculation that Seth confessed to her and that she killed herself jumping off the cliff. Later, when Ariana's pregnancy began to show, there was whispering that she had shoved her sister off the cliff. Much to Ariana's surprise, Seth didn't do the gentlemanly thing. Instead, he boarded a ship and went back out to sea, leaving her to deal with her pregnancy alone. She visited the Widow Hobbs, determined to rid her body of the baby growing inside her, but the Widow Hobbs either refused to help her, or the herbs didn't work. Ariana gave birth to twin girls, one with golden blonde hair, the other with darker locks, just like her and her dead sister. Ariana wouldn't care for the blonde baby, so it was taken away from her to be raised by a relative who was nursing. Within days, the dark-haired baby died, and Ariana lost her mind. She went completely insane. She was a wild woman who attacked anyone who came near her.

"The family called for a doctor from Portland to see if there was anything that could be done. He suggested that she be sent to a sanitarium where they could deal with her. The family refused. Then they tried the Widow Hobbs, but she wouldn't help. She said Ariana was possessed by evil spirits, maybe even the Devil himself, and she would have nothing to do with it. After that, the family just decided to lock Ariana up on the fourth floor. They hired a husband and wife to help care for her. She lived for years up there, and the family tried to pretend she no longer existed, but it was hard to do because Ariana would scream for hours on end. Then, one day, the screaming stopped, and Ariana was dead."

Emma looked over at Reagan. The girl's face was drawn, and her mouth was hanging slightly open. The emotions ranged from anger to disbelief.

"So, you are telling me she now haunts the house, and she is looking for revenge or something?"

"I am telling you that you must have really pissed off that ghost." Reagan shook her head in denial.

"What have I done? I'm living at Willow's house and staying in Adelaide's room. Why is that a problem?"

"It's not that you are here. It's that you are young, attractive, and strong enough of a presence to bring Seth back. You found yourself attracted to him, and apparently, him to you." Reagan blushed and squirmed uncomfortably. Chase gave her a reassuring squeeze.

"Now you are saying Seth isn't real? That a ghost gave me a necklace? A ghost fought off the birds? A ghost kissed me?" She stopped and looked up at Chase, guilt written all over her face. "Just to make things clear, I didn't know you then."

"I know. No worries." Despite his words, Chase looked uncomfortable, but he squeezed her hand gently.

"Seth has a very strong presence, and it seems he has some unfinished business. Ariana has always been a presence in the house, but she has been quiet for years, in the background. She caused trouble in the past, but not recently. I think you coming here has stirred things up. I'm not sure what is going to happen, but I feel you are in some very real danger."

"What can she do to me, really? She doesn't really exist. I mean, I know that you say she is a ghost, but she can't hurt me, can she?"

"What are those?" Chase asked, as he pointed to the punctures in her neck where the cat pierced her with his claws in the night.

"That's where the cat scratched me. You know that. I had the bad dream, and when I woke up, the cat was laying on my chest."

"Your dream was about Ariana hurting you, right?" asked Chase. "And then the cat was hurting you."

"Are you telling me that the cat is Ariana?"

"Reagan, hasn't Willow been telling you since you arrived not to go on the fourth floor?"

"I didn't. I never went there."

"I know you didn't, but you did let something out from there. Something that had been locked in that place for over a hundred and fifty years."

"Because Ariana died up there, you think her ghost has been trapped up there?" Reagan shook her head in disbelief.

"Not only did she die up there, but she stayed up there."

"Wait, you mean she wasn't buried or anything? Are you telling me they left her body up there to rot? That's disgusting. Honestly, that had to get really disgusting, didn't it?"

"That's the strange thing. Her body didn't decompose. At least, that's the story. There was never a smell. The family shut the door and forbid anyone to go up there. They just pretended that nothing had ever happened, and they went on with their lives."

"Wait, you said Ariana caused trouble some years back. What happened?"

"Your father," said Emma

"What do you mean, my father?"

"You remember the story of when your dad's collie died? The day your dad almost drowned?" asked Emma, putting down her knitting. Reagan nodded.

"No one knows what really happened, except for Willow and me. Your father had met a beautiful girl down on the rocks at the ocean. He would go down there daily to see her. Willow kept telling him that something wasn't right with this picture, but he wouldn't listen. Then one day, I don't know why, but he realized that something didn't add up. He said he met the girl's sister, and she warned him to stay away because the girl wasn't well. He acknowledged that the house held, what he called memories, but he had a hard time accepting the fact that spirits from the past haunted his home. Anyhow, the more Willow tried to warn him about the girl he was seeing, the more bad things were happening to her. She was burned by a candle that just toppled for no reason off a shelf. She fell down the basement stairs, and one time, she was bitten by a wolf under the dining room table."

"So, you're saying that Ariana did these things? But wasn't she locked up?"

Emma poured more tea in her cup and rose to refill Reagan's. Reagan shook her head impatiently, urging Emma to go on. Emma settled back resigned to finishing the sordid story.

"Over the years she had been gaining power. She was able to reach beyond her attic prison. One day, your dad confronted the woman on the beach. He insisted that she go into town with him, that she go anywhere with him other than the rocks, and if she didn't, he could no longer see her. The woman flew into a rage and pushed your father off of the rocks. He lost his balance and fell into the ocean. The seas were high that day, and he was having trouble keeping his head above water. His collie jumped in to try to save him. The dog managed to pull him to shore, but the dog had gotten too much salt water in his lungs. The poor thing died, and your dad died a little, too. He cursed the girl, he cursed the house, and he cursed the town. He stayed long enough to graduate high school, then he left and never came back. Willow was devastated, and so were their parents."

"Why did they stay? Why didn't they leave that cursed place? How can Willow still live there?"

"Because that is her home, your home. Your family has lived there for generations. Your ancestors have been married there, babies have been born there, and people have grown old and died there. That house has been filled with many, many happy memories. Adelaide's spirit walks that house and people have enjoyed her goodwill for years. Ariana has just gained strength in the last forty years or so."

"Isn't there a way to get rid of her?"

"Yes, but Willow has never wanted it done."

"Why the hell not? After what happened to her brother?"

"Because Willow understands the pain that Ariana felt. I think she feels sorry for her. Ariana was always second fiddle to the beautiful, kind, and graceful Adelaide. She didn't feel as loved, and she was an outcast. Willow grew up much the same way. She didn't have a sister that she lived in the shadow of, but Willow was always a little different. Because she's artistic, she didn't fit in well with this tight knit, conservative community. Her peers made fun of her, and she spent much of her life feeling very lonely. Now, she is a recluse, with very few close friends. Cora Rose and Willow have a grudging respectful relationship, and I have become friends with Willow over the years. I think Willow prefers the house's ghosts to people. She understands them, and they are part of her world and her history. My guess is you have always had friends, so this would be pretty hard for you to understand."

Reagan thought about it for a few minutes as the three of them sat in a companionable silence.

"Honestly, I don't know what to think anymore," said Reagan. "My head is spinning, I'm confused, and I just feel like curling up and going to sleep."

"That's not a bad idea. Your mind is overwhelmed, and you need to heal, both physically and emotionally. Also, the tea and the incense have calmed you, and your body is responding to its relaxing powers. Why don't you curl up on the couch and take a nap? Chase and I will start dinner so when you wake up, there will be something to eat. After that, we will go over to the house and pick up a some of your things. You are going to stay in our guest room for a couple of days. Does that sound like a good idea?" Reagan nodded gratefully. Chase stood up and Reagan stretched out on the couch. He covered her carefully with the blanket and kissed her cheeks. Within seconds, Reagan was fast asleep.

CHAPTER 22

*R*eagan woke to the smell of chicken soup simmering. She opened her eyes and saw Emma turn to look at her, dusting her flour covered hands on her jeans.

"How are you feeling?" asked Emma as she crossed the floor toward Reagan.

"Hungry," Reagan replied as she sniffed the air appreciatively.

"The food will be ready in a bit. Can I get you anything right now?"

"I would like water, but I can get it. Can I help you with anything in the kitchen?"

Emma appraised her and nodded. She showed Reagan how to roll the dough she had mixed and how to cut it into dumplings. Once they had them all cut, Emma dusted them again with flour, then turned the fire up higher under the chicken stock. The fragrant herbs that simmered in the soup filled the room. Once the pot was at a rolling boil, they carefully loaded the dumplings into the stock. Reagan stirred the soup gently, forcing the dumplings apart so they would cook separately.

"Can I ask you a couple of questions?" Reagan asked Emma.

"Of course, Reagan, you can ask me anything, and I won't lie to you. You must remember that the truths I tell you might be hard for you to accept. Deal?"

"Deal. Okay, so why do you have Ariana's journal?"

"I wondered when you would ask that. The Widow Hobbs was my ancestor. Just like your family has lived in the big house on the cliff, my family has lived here in this cottage. Each of us lives with our own curses. Our family has only ever produced girls, and our husbands all passed early. I am the first to have produced a son. I was hoping that meant the curse had passed, and that my husband would not suffer the same fate as all the husbands in this family, but it was not to be." Emma swiped her flour-covered hands on a towel, taking a minute to compose herself. "The gossip about town is our family was cursed because the Widow Hobbs had practiced black magic. They claim this is why Ariana went insane. Our family has tried for generations to swing the town's perception of the healing arts. People only wanted to come to us under the cover of darkness, afraid of being ostracized, even though everyone came to us for help. At least now I am respected and loved in this town, so slowly, I think the curse is being broken. I just wish it would have happened before Chase's father died." Emma was quiet for a minute. Reagan waited patiently.

"Anyhow, the Widow Hobbs helped to deliver Ariana's babies, and then cared for her in the beginning as she became more and more mentally ill. At one point, Ariana gave the book to the widow for safe keeping. I think she wanted her side of the story told. When Ariana spiraled into the depths of madness, the Widow Hobbs refused to come back to the house, but the book has been in our family for ages, and we have protected it as it was trusted to us for safe keeping. You said you had two questions. What is the other one?"

"I understand that you think Adelaide haunts the house, and that Ariana takes the form of the cat. But what about the wolves? I mean, there were wolves under the table. I saw them. They snapped at me." Reagan shuddered at the memory.

"I think the wolves are something completely different, but Ariana has learned to harness them and use them. For centuries, the native people indigenous to this land have had a legend about a pack of spirit wolves. There are a couple of places in that house which offer a portal to places and things we don't understand. Under the dining room table is one. There is also one down in the basement."

"The room with the big locked door."

"Yes, you want to stay away from that place. I have had to cleanse that many, many times."

"Cleanse? What are you talking about?"

"I purified the house. We will do it again tonight. When we go over to get some of your things, we will burn sage and hang rosemary wreaths. It will help keep things under control." Reagan looked dubious but decided the only thing she could do right now was to trust Emma.

After dinner, Emma, Chase, and Reagan climbed in Emma's truck. Wiley jumped in the bed, eager to go for a ride. The drive over the Willow's house was silent, each contemplating their own thoughts. Chase clasped Reagan's hand, gritting his teeth at times because Reagan unconsciously gripped his hand to the point of almost crushing his fingers. Outwardly, she tried to look calm, but her hands betrayed her fears.

Once they got to the house, Wiley jumped out and stayed glued to Reagan's side. As they approached the porch, Emma lit a twist of sage and let the smoke curl up into the rafters. Chase took Reagan's key and unlocked the front door. Reagan's heart was pounding against the walls of her chest. As they walked through the kitchen, the sage burning fragrantly, Wiley trotted ahead, wagging his tail. He sat in the middle of the kitchen and offered his paw to no one in particular. Emma spoke up.

"I'm sorry Adelaide, if the sage is bothering you. I need to purify the house because Ariana is causing trouble here. Please forgive me for your discomfort."

Reagan looked at Emma in disbelief. This was so weird. Everything she had ever believed in was being shattered in just a couple weeks. She still felt like she was going slightly mad, but she followed along for the ride.

Chase dropped an arm around her shoulders and pulled her close. A door upstairs slammed. Emma moved her way into the dining room. She placed ground sage under each chair at the dining room table, allowing the smoke to curl and fill the space below. As they turned to leave, Wiley wheeled around and sounded a low, deep growl. His hackles raised. His tail grew straight.

"It's okay, Wiley. They are restless and uncomfortable," Emma soothed.

They made their way up the stairs, smudging every room with the sage smoke, Emma muttering soft words under her breath. When they reached Reagan's room Emma stopped at the entrance, then backed up a step. Her eyes flashed with anger, and she motioned for the kids to get behind her. Wiley moved up next to Emma, his teeth bared.

"Mom, what is it?" Chase whispered. He moved closer to his mom, wanting to protect her, but she pressed him back. A cold draft blew from the room, forcing the sage smoke back into their faces. The burning end glowed brightly, then faded. Emma quickly lit the sage again, coaxing it into a brighter flame.

She reached into the market bag that hung from her shoulder and extracted a rosemary wreath. An angry hiss came from under the bed. Wiley entered the room, stiff-legged, growling louder, his lips curled on top of his nose. Emma moved sideways into the room, Chase and Reagan following. Emma motioned for them to move around the perimeter, leaving the path from the bed to the hallway clear. As the sage smoke filled the room, the hiss turned into a low growling yowl. The cat was angry. Emma moved to the other side of the bed and reached the rosemary wreath out in front of her. The cat hissed again, low and throaty. Emma pushed the wreath under the bed and threw ground sage leaves under for good measure. Then she thrust the still smoldering sage bundle under. The cat howled and ran for the hallway and up the stairs to the fourth floor. A door slammed, and a woman screamed. Then all was quiet.

Reagan gathered the things she needed to spend the next couple of nights at Emma's house. Chase stayed by her side the entire time. Reagan was surprised at how frightened she was to go down the hall to the bathroom to get her toiletries. Emma sensed her hesitation and went with her, carrying the smoking sage bundle. Before they went back downstairs, Emma hung a rosemary wreath on Reagan's door and shut it firmly.

"I don't know if I will ever be able to sleep in there again," Reagan said, sadly. "I loved that room."

"Trust me. You will. You need to learn to coexist with all things in life, not just the pleasant things."

"Yeah, well that may take a while. Is Ariana gone for good? What happened to her?"

"No, I am afraid not. She is subdued, but she is no longer locked up on the fourth floor. She has been freed, and I am really not sure how to confine her again. I will have to think about it. You have some protection down here. These floors have been purified, but the fourth floor has not. On the other hand, don't you think she should have a safe place of her own?" Emma reached out and brushed a strand of hair from Reagan's eyes, looking at her earnestly.

"But she was evil. She killed Adelaide."

"True, but there are two sides to every story. This is not the place to discuss it, but we will. In the meantime, think about how we treat people today with mental illness, and imagine how those same people would be treated a hundred and fifty years ago. It's not a pretty thought."

Reagan got quiet and realized that Emma had a point. Still,

Ariana was pure evil, and she didn't seem to have reformed after death.

They carried Reagan's things down the stairs. Everything was quiet in the dining room. Leaving the sconce light on in the kitchen, Chase locked up, handing Reagan the key. Emma hung another rosemary wreath on the kitchen door, and they left for the cottage.

CHAPTER 23

*R*eagan spent the next two days at the cottage. She helped Emma make soap and tend to the garden. In the early morning, she helped to harvest lavender blossoms so Emma could make lavender oil and lavender salve. Wiley and Griff stayed close by Reagan's side, keeping a constant watch over her. Chase went to work at the drugstore, coming home in the evenings to help with dinner. After the dinner dishes were cleaned, they sat together on the patio and watched the sun set over the bog.

In the evening of the second day, the phone rang. Willow was home and wanted to check on Reagan and Wiley. Emma assured her everyone was fine.

"Willow, do you need me to run Wiley over to you this evening? I think it would be better for Reagan to stay here one more night, but I know you would like for Wiley to be with you."

"No, that's okay. I will stop by and pick him up. Now that Cora Rose isn't here, there isn't any damn food in the house. I need to pick up something for breakfast tomorrow. I noticed you did a cleansing. The rosemary wreaths are a nice touch. A little feminine for my taste, but if they will do the trick, I welcome them. Thanks for your help."

"You're welcome. If there is anything else you need, just let me know."

"What I needed was for Reagan not to meddle in things that were none of her business. Now that Ariana is out, things will be more difficult around here."

"Willow, it's not Reagan's fault, and you know it. She only did what any decent human being would do and that was help a distressed animal."

"I know, but damn, I can't find the cat, and I am not sure what to do about Ariana. Adelaide is restless as hell, and things just feel off kilter."

"Adelaide is upset because of the cleansing. Just go about your business and see how things go. I'll talk to Cora Rose and see if I can convince her to come back to cook your breakfast."

Willow snorted her lack of conviction that Emma could work that kind of magic.

"I'll see you in a little bit when I pick up Wiley."

Emma hung up the phone and turned around to see Reagan standing behind her, a tear running down her check. Emma opened her arms and Reagan threw herself into the welcoming hug.

"It's not your fault, honey. Willow knows you were only trying to help, and besides, Willow has lived in that house all of her life. It is not a surprise that this has finally happened. The cleansing should have moved an unwelcome spirit out of those rooms. Ariana should go back upstairs because that area is not contaminated with the sage smoke, and the strong presence of rosemary won't be up there. Willow will spend the night in the house, and she will know if anything is awry." Emma gently lifted Reagan's chin so she could look in her eyes. Reagan's lashes were wet with tears, her face touched with sadness.

"Since you did the smoke thing, does this mean I won't be attacked by sea gulls anymore?"

"No, I'm sorry to say it doesn't. Ariana had the power to control the gulls while her spirit was confined to the fourth floor. If she is up there now, she still has those same powers". Reagan pulled away from Emma, frustrated and frightened. Emma reached for her, smoothing her hair, trying to comfort Reagan with her touch. "This is why it was important for you to wear the starfish pendant, Reagan. Seth made that pendant for Adelaide, and he gave it to you because he knew it would keep you safe from Ariana's mischief."

"But if Seth made it for Adelaide, did he know Ariana was evil?"

"He knew she was a jealous female. I don't think he thought she was evil."

"Do you think Adelaide jumped, fell, or was pushed?"

"I don't like to think poorly of anyone, but I really don't think she jumped, so that leaves falling or being pushed. I hate to say it, but I think Ariana pushed her off the cliff."

"Then why didn't the necklace protect Adelaide. Isn't that why Seth made it?" Reagan moved away from Emma, needing some space. She never believed in this stuff, but now she desperately wanted to believe that the starfish would have protected Adelaide.

"She wasn't wearing it that day. It was her wedding day, and she was wearing a strand of pearls that belonged to her grandmother. They were more fitting for the wedding gown."

Reagan was quiet, thinking how sad it was that Adelaide's life ended while she was so young.

"I know how you feel about Adelaide, how it wasn't fair, but I want you to try to think about Ariana. It can't be easy being trapped in a mind that is mentally ill. No one really knows what kind of hell that is like, unless they live it themselves," said Emma.

Willow stopped by after Reagan had already gone to bed. Wiley reluctantly left Reagan's side to go home with his mistress.

Emma promised Willow again that she would try to convince Cora Rose that she would be safe at the house.

The next morning, Chase drove Reagan back to Willow's. She was nervous when she stepped out of the car, but everything seemed back to normal. Wiley came bounding up to her, his tail wagging in greeting. As they entered the kitchen, they found Willow fighting with a spatula and a skillet, an egg half out of the pan and half on the burner of the stove.

Reagan gently pushed Willow out of the way. She quickly cleaned up the mess and expertly cracked an egg into the skillet. Dropping two pieces of toast into the toaster and warming the slices of ham in another skillet filled with butter, Reagan delivered Willow a reasonable breakfast almost as efficiently as Cora Rose would have done.

"There aren't any blueberry muffins," Willow grumbled. Chase looked at Reagan with a twinkle in his eye. She turned to confront Willow and realized both Willow and Chase were laughing at her. It dawned on her that it was as close to a compliment as she was going to get from her aunt.

"I'm going out to the barn to work. Let me know if you need anything, and thanks for breakfast." Willow grabbed a Pepsi out of the fridge and left the kitchen.

Chase and Reagan carried her things up to her bedroom. She hesitated as she went in the room, but the slight scent of sage reassured her.

"Do you think everything is going to be okay?" Reagan asked Chase, nervously,

"I think it will. Mom would never let you come back here if she thought you were in danger."

"I know you're right. It doesn't feel scary, but still, I feel like something isn't really resolved."

"No, it probably isn't, but I don't think Ariana or the cat is going to bother you. Also, you have the sage mom gave you, right? You know how to smudge your room and anywhere else you need to, so if you feel like there is an unwanted presence, light some sage and let it smoke. I hate to say this, but I have to get to work. You're going to be okay, right?"

"Yes, I'm going to be just fine."

"What do you plan on doing today?"

"I don't know. I might call Olivia and see what she's up to."

"That sounds like a good idea. Have fun, and I'll talk to you later." With that, Chase gathered her in his arms. "I need to know you're okay." Reagan tilted her chin upward and looked him steadily in the eyes.

"I. Will. Be. Just. Fine." Chase leaned down and kissed her lips, sweetly at first, but then more urgently. Reagan leaned into him and kissed him back, pressing against his body. Somewhere in the house, a cat growled, low and menacingly.

Reagan woke to the smell of bacon frying. She stretched under her covers and smiled. That smells good, she thought. Then she sat bolt upright. Bacon. That could only mean that Cora Rose was back. She grabbed her robe and slipped her feet into her slippers, yanked open her door and flew down the stairs. She could hear Willow and Cora Rose talking in the kitchen.

"Scared the crap out of that girl, I tell ya," It sounded like Willow's voice.

"Hell, scared the crap out of me," replied Cora Rose. "I wasn't coming back, but Emma assures me that things will be okay. I guess I really don't have to worry, 'cause Ariana doesn't have a beef with me, but Reagan must have really pissed her off good."

"Not just Reagan," growled Willow. "A whole damn kiln load of plates blew up in the kiln the other day. That has Ariana's signature all over it."

"Why is she mad at you? You didn't do anything."

"She's always been angry with me because I favor Adelaide, but she knows I have protected her, even though she should have been destroyed years ago. She knows she's on thin ice."

"You always have had a soft spot for her," grumbled Cora Rose.

"That I have. Good morning, Reagan."

"Good morning. Hi, Cora Rose. I am so happy you're back. Breakfast smells amazing."

"Grab some while it's hot so's I'm not wasting my time here, and I made you coffee, so your day should be complete."

"I'm really sorry about things, Cora Rose. I should never have..."

"Let it go, Reagan. It was bound to happen."

"Willow, I heard you say Ariana should have been destroyed years ago. What did you mean by that?"

"That is something I would rather not talk about." Willow raised her eyebrows at Reagan, challenging her to cross the line.

"Okay, Aunt Willow. I'll let it go."

"Hmmpf, the girl is a quick learner," said Cora Rose, and she pulled two blueberry pies out of the oven. "Are you going to see your boyfriend this afternoon?"

Reagan could feel the red flush creep up her neck and flood her cheeks.

"I'll take that as a yes," teased Cora Rose. "Take one of these pies over to Emma to thank her for the cleansing."

"Okay. Thank you, I'll do that. I know Emma and Chase will really appreciate it."

"Just tell her I expect the cleansing to keep working because we don't know where Ariana is spending her time. It makes me jumpy, and I'm not cleaning the upstairs. Bring your sheets down when you want them washed, and I will give you the fresh sheets to put on your bed."

"Wait a minute," said Willow, "Does the same thing go for me?"

"Yes ma'am. Until I'm certain Ariana is under control, I'm not setting foot upstairs. Now eat your breakfast so I can clean up and get the hell out of here."

Willow smiled at Reagan. All was right with the world again.

"What are you going to do today?" asked Willow.

"I was hoping to run out and see Mr. Whitstock's puppies." Reagan was surprised to see a melancholy look on her aunt's face.

"Whitstock has the finest puppies around. It's amazing he is still breeding dogs at his age. They're a lot of work, but I am glad he can still keep up with them. It will be a sad day when there are no more Whitstock puppies around."

"I would like to have one," said Reagan, a little surprised as the words left her mouth. She had toyed with the idea, but now the thought of having her own puppy was like a live thing in her brain.

"Why not get one?" asked Willow, looking steadily into her niece's eyes.

"I don't know how my mom would feel about that. I mean, we've never talked about a dog. I don't know the first thing about raising a puppy."

"Well, I do, and it's not that hard. It just takes commitment."

"I can do that."

"You can't get tired of the novelty and just quit."

"I know. I think I am willing to do that. I love Wiley, and I can't imagine leaving him when I go at the end of the summer. He is always with me, by my side, protecting me."

"Yeah, he sure is. My own dog has abandoned me for the pretty, young thing." Willow teased in a rare warm moment.

"So, don't puppies need to be potty-trained?"

"Of course, they do."

"Don't they need to go outside at night?" Reagan asked, carefully.

"Yes, they do."

"Well, you say it's not safe outside after dark. What would I do about the night time part?"

"First, you have to get your mom to say yes to the puppy. Then we will discuss night potty issues. I have raised many dogs, and we will figure out the logistics if your mom agrees. Now, I have to get to work, and you need to put some clothes on if you are going to head over to Whitstock's. I don't think his heart would handle a girl in her pajamas showing up at his place."

"Hi, Mom. Thanks for calling me back. I just really needed to hear your voice."

"I'm sorry it took so long for me get back to you. I miss you so much, honey. Are you okay? You sound really stressed. You were supposed to be spending a relaxing summer reading library books."

"I have been, but maybe I should stop reading horror stories. They're keeping me up at night," Reagan joked.

"Seriously, Reagan. What's wrong?"

"This place is just weird, Mom." Reagan hated being evasive, but she wasn't going to tell her mom all about the ghosts. Not only was her mom halfway around the world, but that woman definitely didn't believe in ghosts. It would just complicate things. "I think I am just missing my friends, and there are creepy things about this place, so I let my imagination run away with me."

"Is there anything good about the place? Anything you can tell me that will stop me from feeling so incredibly guilty?"

"I met a guy. He's really nice."

"Ah, nothing better than a summer romance. I will just get

home in time to pick up the pieces when the two of you break up because you have to go home." Her mother teased.

"Well, if you're feeling the right amount of guilt, I can help you appease that."

"Oh really, what do you have in mind? What do you want?"

"A dog."

"Wait, what?"

"I want a dog, please? The breeder that Daddy bought his collie from is still breeding dogs, and he has some collie puppies. Chase is going to take me over so I can see them. Is there any way I can have a puppy? Please?"

"I don't think we have the time to talk about this right now."

"Mom, I am home alone a lot. It would be good for me to have a dog. I will be responsible for him and everything."

"I know, I know, and you will teach him not to bark, right?"

"What?"

"Never mind... How are you going to pay for this dog? They aren't cheap, and there are vet bills and food."

"I know, but I have money from Daddy in my bank account. You always say that I am frugal and never spend money on myself. Please let me do this. I love Wiley, and I hate that I will leave him at the end of summer. I would love to have my own dog."

"Oh, what the hell. Go ahead. Just remember, you will be responsible for him for a long time. And Reagan, pick a good puppy. There is an art to it, from what I understand."

"Don't worry, Chase and Emma will help me. It's all good."

Chase walked up to the bench in the garden where Reagan was still sitting after hanging up from her mom.

"Good news?" he asked.

"Yes and no. Mom still isn't able to come home, but she said yes to the puppy. I get to pick out my very own dog." She hugged Chase impulsively.

"Mom has to deliver some more salve to Mr. Whitstock. You

can come along and talk to him about what pups he might have available."

"How soon will she be ready to go?" asked Reagan, jumping off the bench, excited to get moving.

"Whoa there, tiger. You aren't even ready for a dog, yet. You need a few things to help make the pup feel at home. If you want, we can run to the store and pick up what you need, but we should call Mr. Whitstock and see if he has any pups ready to go to homes yet."

A quick call to Mr. Whitstock was the assurance Reagan needed to go ahead and buy the things she would need to make her puppy happy after leaving the comfort of its mother. After letting Emma know they were going, Chase and Reagan jumped in his car to head to the store.

"I'm glad to have you back, Reagan. You scared me," said Chase as he reached over to squeeze her hand.

"I scared myself."

"Yeah, well for a minute there, I thought that you would never start talking again. You just stared into space, weeping. I'm really glad you're back." Chase brushed a strand of hair out of Reagan's eyes.

"I have to be honest, Chase. I am still afraid at the house. I'm not jumping on getting a puppy because it will keep my mind off of the things that scare me, but I will enjoy having another companion. Wiley is wonderful, but to have a dog of my own has to be even better."

"Well, just remember, you will be this puppy's protector for quite a while. He will not be old enough to protect you for a long time."

"I know, but I bet he barks when something is scary, right?"

"I'm not trying to bust your bubble, I want you to know what you're getting into, not to mention the responsibility of owning a puppy. You need to protect him from danger as much as he needs to protect you."

Reagan leaned over and lightly kissed his cheek, careful not to distract him too much while he was driving. He laughed and reached over to grab her hand. "I can see you only have the puppy on your mind right now.

"The thing is, my rational mind keeps telling me that all this isn't real, that I have just been imagining everything. I don't believe in this stuff, I never have. Don't get me wrong, you and your mom have given me convincing arguments, and the other day it all sounded plausible, but today, I'm having a hard time accepting everything. Even those stupid wolves. My mind just doesn't want to accept that there was really something there, and that they really snapped at me."

"Reagan, you're smart. You have a logical mind, and you don't just believe something because someone tells you a story. You are going to have to come to grips with it yourself. It's okay for you to be skeptical. It's even okay for you to not believe, as long as you protect yourself and not allow yourself to get hurt. I wish you still had that starfish necklace."

"Even though Seth made it," Reagan teased.

"Even though it galls me, yes, even though Seth gave it to you."

Just then Reagan gasped.

"What's wrong?" Chase glanced at her, but still tried to keep his eyes on the road.

"When Seth gave me the starfish, I thought it looked familiar, but I couldn't place it. Now I realize where I saw it before. Adelaide was holding it in one of the old photographs, and your mom said she hadn't seen it in years. Explain that!"

"I can't. I don't know when my mom would have seen the necklace, or anything else about it. I just wish you could find it."

"That's what is so weird. It was on my neck when I went to sleep that night. When I had that bad dream and woke up, and the cat was sitting on my chest, that's when the necklace disappeared. The cat must have taken it. Is that possible? It was supposed to protect me from the likes of Ariana, so how could the cat have been able to take it? Wouldn't she have an aversion to it like Ariana does?"

"I don't know how it works. Maybe the cat isn't truly Ariana. Maybe it just does her bidding. Maybe she is still locked upstairs, but she is controlling the cat from there."

"All I know," said Reagan, "is my head is spinning, and I don't have an answer for anything."

"Well, give it a rest for now. There is nothing you can do about it at this moment. We will get the stuff your new puppy is going to need, and then we will worry about this other stuff when we need to and not before."

Reagan nodded her head in agreement. She was done thinking about ghosts and mean cats. She was going to concentrate on her new puppy.

Together, they picked out a food dish and water bowl set, a bed, and a small collar and leash. Reagan wanted to buy food, but Chase told her that she would have to feed the puppy the same thing he had been eating. When they arrived back at the cottage, Emma met them at the car.

"I have the things Mr. Whitstock needed. Are you ready? Your mom said yes to the puppy, right?"

"Yes, she did. I am so excited."

CHAPTER 24

*W*here is Sammy?" Reagan asked as she burst into the kitchen.

"What do you mean?" asked Willow as she poured syrup on her pecan waffles.

"He wasn't in his crate this morning. Did you come in my room and let him out to go potty?"

"No, I let him out around one in the morning, but that was the last time."

"Did you shut the crate and latch it?"

"Of course, I did, Reagan. I have raised a lot of pups. I double check the latch every time. Cora Rose, did you see Sammy?" asked Willow.

Cora Rose turned around with a worried look on her face. She shook her head and glanced nervously toward the dining room. Reagan paled. It had been so quiet in the house lately that she hadn't thought about the wolves.

"Relax," said Willow. "I'm sure Sammy is just fine. I had a pup one time who could work the tray out of the bottom of a crate and slide right out. How he got himself so flat, I will never know, but he did it. I'm sure Sammy is up to the same mischief. I will look inside. Why don't you look outside, although I can't imagine he could have gotten out of the house."

Reagan ran upstairs to get her shoes. She looked carefully at the crate. The bottom tray was pulled part way out, and Sammy's stuffed squeaky duck lay outside the cage. Maybe he did sneak out last night. She laced up her shoes and called for him. She didn't hear the low chuckle that echoed down the stairs from the fourth floor.

As she entered the kitchen, she came upon Willow coming up from the first-floor basement.

"Any sign of him?" asked Reagan, anxiously.

"Nothing," said Willow.

"Well, there's a sign in here," grumbled Cora Rose. Willow and Reagan followed Cora Rose's voice into the library. There, on the hardwood floor was a small puddle of puppy pee. "You'd better find him soon, or there is going to be a lot more of these places for you to clean up." Cora Rose raised her eyebrow at Reagan.

"I'm sorry," Reagan mumbled as she went into the kitchen to get a rag and the spray bottle of white vinegar they had readied for such incidents.

"You clean that while we keep on looking."

Reagan wiped up the urine and sprayed the spot with the vinegar. Her cell phone rang just as she was finishing.

"Hey Reagan, what's wrong?" asked Chase, worry filling his voice. Reagan still wasn't used to the fact that he knew when she needed him.

"Sammy is gone. His crate was empty this morning. The tray is pulled slightly out. I think he escaped. We found some pee in the library. Cora Rose is not happy."

"I expect not. Have you checked the whole house?"

"Willow is looking in the house. I'm heading outside just in case he somehow got out."

"Where's Wiley?"

"You know, I have no idea. He's not around either."

"Well, you might find the two of them together. Keep looking. I'm going to head over to help you. I don't have to go to work today, so I have the time."

"You have to stop doing that," said Reagan.

"Doing what?" said Chase, innocently.

"You know what... anticipating what I am going to say."

"Get used to it. Besides, it saves time. I'll see you in a few minutes."

Reagan put the cleaning supplies away and went outside calling for Sammy and Wiley. She checked under the porch then headed out to the orchard.

"Sammy... Sammy... Wiley. Here boy!" Reagan called repeatedly. There was no sign of them in the orchard. She wandered over to the barn, but the doors were shut tightly.

Crossing the meadow, she kept calling, but there was nothing. She found herself on the path to the cliff. She hadn't been there since the day of the gull attack, the day Chase carried her in his arms up the cliff and away from this place. She hesitated at the top where the trail led down toward the ocean.

"Sammy," Reagan called. "Sammy!" She stood there, listening. "Sammy!" she called again. Then she heard it, a slight, faint whimper over the sound of the ocean. "Sammy!" she screamed. Reagan started down the cliff path calling as she hurried along. As she rounded the cliff to the rocks, she saw her puppy, lying on his side on a slanting rock, waves crashing up and around his still body.

"Sammy!" Reagan ran over the last of the rocks, trying to get to her dog. He lay perfectly still. Another wave crashed, covering his body, the receding wave pulling him toward the ocean. "No," she screamed as she jumped forward, trying to cover his body with hers. Another wave broke, and Reagan felt two strong arms push her. She fell back off the rock, dropping into the ocean three feet below.

Her head slipped under the water, the cold shock making her

gasp. Her mouth filled with the salty ocean. Coughing, she kicked her way to the surface. Another wave hit her and slammed her into the rocks. Reagan fought against the strong pull of the receding tide. Her wet clothes drug her downward. Again, Reagan struggled her way to the surface and grabbed a bite of air. She tried to get a second breath, but she wasn't quick enough. Again, salt water poured into her mouth. Her body, chilling down rapidly, was being battered against the rocks, and her arms were feeling heavy. Over and over again, Reagan fought the relentless waves and the pulling undercurrent. As hard as she tried, she was losing the fight to stay at the surface. She was just so tired, and it would be so easy just to stop.

"No!" Chase's voice exploded in her head. She opened her eyes in the salty water. "You fight, damn you! You keep fighting! I'm coming to get you." His voice was everywhere. Her head was completely under water, and her legs were being dragged along the rocky bottom. She kicked again, fighting to break through the surface. Again, a wave hit her, slamming her head into a rock. Everything went dark.

Reagan dreamt she felt arms around her. She looked into Seth's sad eyes as he held her close. Her hair floated out away from her in silky tendrils, and her body seemed weightless. Seth kissed her forehead gently, then slipped the starfish necklace around her neck. Looking at her one more time, he chastely kissed her lips then lifted her high above his head. Reagan's body floated upward, breaking through the surface of the ocean, the sun glinting off her hair and her starfish.

Strong arms pulled Reagan onto the rocks and gathered her close. A piercing scream rang though the air. Lips locked over hers and began to breathe life into her body.

Reagan looked on from above. She saw Chase working to bring her back. She watched Willow clutching Wiley by his neck and Emma rubbing Sammy's tiny body, trying to pull the life back into his soul. She turned her attention from the scene and looked to the ocean. There she saw Seth, his face at peace, rising from the ocean depths. The sun was dazzling as he disappeared into its rays. A woman cried out, the anguish in her voice betraying the pain in her soul.

Reagan coughed and sputtered up sea water. Chase rolled her gently to her side so she wouldn't choke all over again. When he was sure she was breathing on her own, he gathered her into his arms and once again carried her up the cliff.

CHAPTER 25

I should burn down the house."

"That would be rash. You mustn't let Ariana win this battle."

"She nearly killed Reagan. She killed my brother. Nothing was the same after she drowned him."

"Shh, Willow. Reagan and Chase will hear you."

Willow lowered her voice.

"I should have let you destroy her the last time. She has just gotten stronger, and now I don't know what's going to happen. Seth has left this plane. Adelaide and Ariana are now alone, without hope of sharing existence with him," said Willow.

"Adelaide can go now. She has no reason to be bound here. Seth has redeemed himself, so he is free. I would assume she will follow," Emma mused.

"That leaves us with that witch, Ariana, and we don't know what she has in store for us."

Chase and Reagan walked in to the cottage living room.

"Ah, you're awake," said Emma. "Can I get you anything?"

"Could I please have some peppermint tea?" asked Reagan quietly. Chase tucked her onto the couch with a woolen throw around her shoulders and moved to the kitchen to help his mom make some tea. He was still scared and angry.

"Calm yourself, Chase. You won't do anyone any good by being angry." Emma whispered.

"I know, but you could have stopped this years ago, and you didn't," hissed Chase. Emma shot him a warning glance.

Reagan interrupted, her voice strong and determined. "It doesn't take second sight to know that something is going on and being discussed here behind my back. I am so done with everything about this place, but most of all, I am done with secrets, so if anyone wants to start talking, I am willing to listen. If you all aren't going to talk, then I'm not going to stay. I will drive myself home to Ohio and deal with my mother's anger when she returns. It will be child's play after what I've been through."

Emma shot a meaningful glance at Willow, but before she could say anything, Reagan spoke up again.

"No one needs anyone else's permission to speak up. It's time to come clean about everything, and I mean now." Chase sat down next to Reagan and nodded his head in complete agreement with her.

At that moment, headlights briefly lighted the cottage before turning toward the soap shed. The lights turned off and a car door slammed. Emma opened the door and stepped out onto the porch. When Mr. Whitstock stepped into the cottage carrying Sammy, Reagan jumped up from the couch and took the puppy from his arms.

"Is he going to be okay?" Reagan asked.

"The vet checked him over and said he's going to be fine. I fed him for you, and he has been outside. He is a very tired puppy and just needs some rest."

"Thanks, Roger for taking care of him and bringing him back. What do I owe you?" said Willow.

"Nothing," said Whitstock, gruffly. "I'm just glad this one turned out a hell of a lot better than the last time. I'll be seeing you ladies. Chase." With that, Whitstock left, giving Reagan a wink on the way out.

Reagan buried her nose in Sammy's soft fur. She took a deep breath of the warm, puppy smell, and stroked his soft ears. Sammy lay down, curling into her lap, and was sleeping in an instant. Reagan smiled down at her puppy, then lifted her eyes to Willow and Emma. Her hands rose to touch the starfish hanging around her neck. It gave her the confidence she needed.

"Spill it," she said. "Come clean, now," she ordered

"My ancestors have always had healing powers and second sight. Usually, they used their powers for good, but often, the people didn't understand. Many, many generations ago, my ancestors were hung, and back in Europe, were even burned at the stake as witches." Emma's eyes held pain as she talked about those atrocities. Griff got up from in front of the fireplace and sat in front of his mistress, leaning into her, whining softly. She reached her hand down and softly scratched his ears. Willow took this moment to excuse herself. She said she was heading back to the house to make sure everything was closed up.

"You know the story of Ariana and Widow Hobbs. You know she tried to help with the birth of the babies. She also tried to care for Ariana when she began her descent into the hell of mental illness, but Etta Hobbs recognized the evil that had taken over Ariana. It wasn't just mental illness that ailed her. True evil lived in that girl, so Etta washed her hands of the whole thing and abandoned Ariana and her family.

"Your family begged Etta to exorcise the wickedness in Ariana, but Etta refused. All of our ancestors understood the danger of dabbling in the dark arts or confronting the evil one. Too many times we had suffered the consequences, so Etta never set foot on the property again.

"When Ariana died, again the family asked the widow to come and cleanse the house. They were terrified to go onto the fourth floor to retrieve the body. Again, Etta refused.

"Years passed, and the family learned to live with the hauntings. Adelaide wasn't a problem, and, at the time, Ariana was weak. The door to the fourth floor remained closed.

"Generations lived and died in the house, and everything was pretty quiet, except for the hairbrushes and trinkets that were moved and chairs that rocked. Often, there was mysterious singing in different parts of the house. No one approached the fourth floor. Anyone who got close described a cold feeling of dread in their soul." Emma cleared her throat, preparing herself to tell the rest of the story, that hard part.

"Then there were a brother and sister who were born in the house, your dad and Willow. Their parents allowed them to run kind of wild and explore at will. Wolf and Willow came upon my house on the bog, and we became fast friends. My mother was nervous about our relationship. Our families' paths had not crossed since the time of Ariana, but Momma was enlightened and allowed the friendship. We were inseparable." Emma smiled wistfully at the memory.

"We grew up together, playing in that house and on the cliffs. My gift of second sight developed strongly when I was about eight years old, and Willow's ability to connect with the dead started when she reached puberty. Wolf was finding his own interests; sports and girls. He had drifted away from us and wasn't involved in our shenanigans."

"Wait, what?" said Reagan, sitting up straighter.

"Shh," said Chase pulling her closer to him. "Just let her go."

Emma picked up where she left off. "Willow told me about a beautiful woman who sang to her at night. She said the woman was nice, but kind of a ditz. That's when we found Adelaide's journal and read it. I recognized the cover as a match to one my mom had, so Willow and I found that one and read it, too. That's where we learned about Ariana and the whole sordid mess.

"Willow was taken with Ariana. She felt a kinship to her. You see, I was Willow's only friend. At school, she was made fun of. For one thing, she lived in the crazy house, and for another, she was artistic, with a name like Willow and a brother named Wolf. She was doomed. I think for a while Willow suffered a mild depression. Anyway, Willow made it a habit to sit at the top of the stairs next to the door on the fourth floor. She started to talk to Ariana, to connect to her. She was innocently trying to empathize with a tortured spirit, but what she did was awaken the evil. Neither one of us was equipped to deal with what was about to happen.

"When your dad was seventeen, he started talking about a beautiful young girl he met on the beach. We didn't think anything about it, figuring it was just another one of his conquests. Then one night, he said he met another girl he liked. Willow had a bad feeling about what was happening, but Wolf wouldn't listen to her. He was smitten with them both. One night, he and I were sitting at the top of the cliff taking about his newest love interests. He told me when he was with the blonde girl, it was like being in the light. She was sweet and kind, but the dark-haired girl was exciting and exotic. He said she was like playing with fire, and he liked the excitement. I remember being afraid for him, and I told him that. He just laughed at me and teased me about my imagined second sight. What he didn't realize is by that time my second sight was incredibly strong. My mother had been training me in the healing arts, and I had been studying the writings of my ancestors. My mother was unaware of that little detail.

"Then one day, Wolf discovered the two girls were sisters. He realized the dark-haired sister knew the blonde liked him, so she set out to win him. Your dad didn't like the deceit. He told me he was going to break it off with the dark beauty. He was unhappy about it, but Wolf really had a strong sense of what was right and what was wrong." Emma picked up her knitting, but after two dropped stitches, she set it down again. She took a moment to center herself, then went on.

"The fateful day at the rocks, Wolf told the dark-haired girl that they were through, that he didn't like her sneaky ways or how she betrayed her sister. He said he never wanted to see her again. Ariana had gained power from his love and attention. It was all she needed to grow strong. Once again, she was jilted out of a lover because of her sister, and she wasn't going to have it. She used her powers and made your father slip off the rocks and fall into the ocean. If she couldn't have him, no one would. She made him weak, so he couldn't save himself. Scout tried to pull him out of the waves but couldn't. I was with Willow in the house when I got the sense something terrible had happened. I asked Willow if she had ever been up to the fourth floor, and she admitted she had opened the door. All of the sudden I knew Ariana had gained strength and was free, and she was the dark-haired girl Wolf had been mooning about. At that moment, I knew Wolf was dead, and that Ariana had killed him.

"Are you telling me that my father was dead? And you brought him back to life with some hocus pocus? You want me to believe that?". Reagan's voice had taken on a touch of hysteria. Chase moved to hold her, but she threw his arms off. Emma waited patiently for Reagan to digest what she had said. Griff sat in front of Reagan, whimpering softly. The puppy opened his eyes and stretched in Reagan's lap. Her hand dropped to her puppy, and she petted him gently to calm him. It calmed her, too.

"I know that it is hard for you to grasp. I understand it goes against everything you believe in, but I can assure you, everything I have told you is true. I am not going to lie to you."

"But you have been lying to me this whole time. Lying by omission, and so has Chase." She looked at him reproachfully,

"Chase didn't know that part of the story. I'm sure he is as disappointed in me as you are, probably more."

"So, is that why my dad left here and never came back?"

"Yes, your father was haunted by what happened to him. He never got over losing Scout."

"Did he know what you did? Did he know who Ariana was, and I am assuming Adelaide?" Reagan stared at Emma, accusations in her eyes. Emma smiled gently at her, accepting her anger, but loving her still.

"No, he didn't, and we never told him. Although, I'm sure deep inside he knew things were not as they seemed. He refused to think about that day and the possibilities, but as soon as he could leave, he did. When his parents passed away, he begged Willow to leave, just to sell the house and move to Ohio with him, but she refused. He felt she was in danger, but he wasn't sure why. When your father passed, Willow spiraled into a deep depression. I was afraid for her. She became terribly protective of the house and the spirits of Adelaide and Ariana."

"Even after everything Ariana had done? I don't understand that."

"What you don't understand is true forgiveness. Willow has the ability to forgive. It's something that most people can't do, but Willow can. I think she has always been afraid she would end up like Ariana because of her bouts of depression. Willow was terrified of being mentally ill and of the evil that possessed Ariana. What she doesn't realize is her goodness, her ability to forgive, keeps the evil at bay. It's why she can go back to the house and be safe, why she has been able to live there for all these years and not be harmed, and Ariana has recognized that Willow has protected her from harm.

"After what Ariana pulled, I wanted to destroy her. I loved your father. The three of us had grown up together, and I loved him like a brother. I am not as forgiving as Willow, and Ariana tried to destroy him. I read everything I could about how to take her out, how to make her descend into the hell that should be her home. Willow would have none of it, but she did let me exorcise Ariana back to the fourth floor." Emma's eyes flashed with the memory. Chases stared at his mom, never seeing this kind of emotion from her.

"And I let her out," whispered Reagan. "She almost killed Sammy and me. I don't know that I can be forgiving."

"You can bet Willow will be hard pressed to be forgiving now, too. That's why she left, you know. Not only did she not want to hear the story, but she is going to have to come to grips with the fact that her life is now going to change. She knows something has to be done about Ariana, and Adelaide might leave. Willow has lived in that house all her life with those ghosts. They are her family, but you are more important family. You are Wolf's daughter, and what Ariana did is unforgivable."

"What's Willow going to do?" Reagan whispered.

"That remains to be seen," said Emma.

CHAPTER 26

A truck pulled into the driveway. Griff walked to the door and waited in greeting, his tail slowly wagging.

"It's just Willow coming back," Emma said.

The door opened, and Willow walked in followed by Wiley, who seemed strangely subdued. When he saw Reagan, he wagged his tail weakly. Emma stared at Wiley. She had a bad feeling, but she couldn't put her finger on what was wrong. Wiley sniffed the puppy on Reagan's lap and then stretched out in front of the fireplace. Griff joined him as they curled together on the floor.

"I brought Reagan some things," said Willow. "I don't want her back at the house until we clean up the mess we made years ago."

"She's welcome to stay here as long as she needs," said Emma. "You know that, and you know that I will help you any way I can. You just need to say the word. Willow, you are also welcome to stay. There's plenty of room for you, and for Wiley, too."

"I appreciate that, but I need to stay at my house. It's my home and has been for all of my life. I will not be driven from it. Wiley can stay if he wants, or he can come with me."

Wiley lifted his head at the sound of his name. He sighed and got to his feet. He looked old and dejected.

"What's wrong with Wiley?" asked Reagan.

"I really don't know," said Willow. "Emma? Any idea?"

Emma walked over to the dog and lifted his chin, looking deeply into his eyes. The dog held stock still, then wagged his tail slightly.

"He'll be fine, eventually. He feels he didn't protect his people. He is very aware that Reagan nearly died. He's having a hard time with that."

Reagan slid her puppy into Chase's lap and dropped to the floor. She threw her arms around the big Lab and buried her face in his neck. She told him she loved him, and it wasn't his fault. He leaned his solid, boxy face against hers and licked her cheek. Then he crossed over and stood next to Willow, ready to go home with her and protect his mistress.

"Chase, why don't you come with me? That way you can pick up your car and bring it back here. I figure you might need it in the morning. Reagan, is there anything you need Chase to bring back?". Reagan looked through the things that Willow had brought.

"No, I think I have everything I need. Thank you, Willow." She crossed the room and pulled her aunt into a hug. "Aunt Willow, I love you. I know that all of this is hard on you, and I'm sorry." Willow looked extremely uncomfortable and awkwardly returned the hug. Then she motioned for Wiley to follow her as she left for home.

An hour later, Chase pulled back into the driveway and cut the engine. He picked Reagan's library books off the front seat and went into the house.

A black cat with a white slash on its side slid out of the warm car engine compartment and slinked in the shadows. He crept under the front porch steps. Inside, Griff lifted his head from the floor and growled a low, throaty growl. The cat stiffened, then streaked out from under the porch and disappeared into the cranberry bog.

Inside the cottage that night, people and dogs were restless. Nightmares haunted their dreams. Griff paced the floors, feeling that something wasn't right in his world.

Emma got up at two o'clock in the morning and lit some sage incense. Using the black ink made from fox glove, she drew a line across the thresholds of her home and lined each window frame with the tincture. When she reached her son's room she was pulled up short at the chill she felt. The window was opened slightly. She settled her spirit and listened with her soul. Quickly, she lit sage, purifying the room. Satisfied, she closed the window and inked the frame, carefully making a full circle, connecting the lines while softly whispering ancient incantations.

Emma was up first that morning. She heard Sammy whining in his crate, and she smiled as Griff gently pawed her, urging her to get up and help the distressed puppy. She pulled on her robe and slippers and padded quietly into the room where Reagan was sleeping. The puppy sat anxiously at the door to the crate. Reagan was sleeping so soundly that she didn't even stir. Emma glanced down at her, checking to see she was okay. Her face was at peace, her fingers of her right hand clasped tightly around the starfish.

Emma turned and opened the crate. She gathered the collie pup in her arms and scooted quickly to the front door. The puppy quivered with excitement.

"Hang on Sammy, almost there." Griff pushed forward too, and sprang out the door, stopping on the porch to survey his property. When he was certain everything was in order, he hopped down the steps and claimed the big oak tree that shaded the house. Sammy, too young to lift his leg, squatted and did his business. Emma made appropriate "good boy" talk and gave both dogs a homemade puppy biscuit. Emma saw Griff wag his tail as he looked up at the porch. She turned to see Chase coming out of the door. He looked a little rough.

"Tough night?" Emma asked.

"Yeah, I had a lot of bad dreams, but I don't remember them. I know I kept waking up feeling like the world was out of control. How about you? I smelled sage this morning."

"I cleansed the house last night. I feel like something is off kilter, but I don't know what it is. All I know is we are not done. This whole thing is going to come to a head, but I can't see what it is going to be. It's as if my second sight is blocked."

"I feel the same way. My head feels cloudy, like there is a haze in my brain. I think it's because I'm so tired. I'm hungry, too. Do you realize we never ate any dinner last night? I'm starving."

"Watch the dogs, and I'll start breakfast. I think it will be just you and I eating. I think Reagan is going to sleep for a long time, and I think it's important that we let her."

Chase nodded in agreement, and Emma went in to start breakfast. Within a few minutes, thick slices of ham were sizzling in a cast iron skillet. Emma sliced potatoes and dropped them into melted butter seasoned with rosemary. She topped them with onions and set the fire on low for them to cook and brown slowly. Chase came in the door with a basketful of freshly gathered eggs. He grinned at his mom appreciatively.

"That smells great. What are you going to eat?" he teased.

"The question is, what are you going to eat?" asked Reagan as she stepped out of the hall.

"I didn't expect you up," said Emma. "I figured you would sleep well into the afternoon."

"I would have, but the smell of breakfast reminded me I never ate yesterday. I'm starving. Can I help you with anything?" Reagan asked. Emma looked at the girl and smiled.

"No, wait, yes, you can brew tea." Emma was going to tell Reagan to relax, but the girl looked lost. If she had a job to do, she would heal a lot faster.

"Thank you, guys, for taking care of Sammy. I guess I'm not a very good dog mom. I should have set my alarm so I would wake up to let him out."

"Don't worry about it. I was proud of him because he whimpered to go out. He's learning that all he needs to do is tell us when he needs to go outside, and we will take him out to his pee spot. He's a smart pup. He'll be potty-trained in no time."

Reagan poured boiling water into the tea pot and added a scoop of loose tea to the tea ball just as Emma had taught her. The fragrant aroma filled the air, mixing with the sage and making the cottage feel like a sanctuary.

"So, what do we do today?" asked Reagan. "I feel like we should be doing something."

"Right now, the something that you are feeling is uncertainty. To be honest, there is nothing for us to do. We wait for Willow to come back and let us know how her night was. Once we have that information, we can make plans. In the meantime, I have an idea for another soap fragrance. I need to create some new product, so I thought you could help. Would you like that?"

"I would love it."

After the breakfast dishes were cleaned, Reagan and Emma gathered the supplies to make a batch of soap. Chase said he needed to mow the lawn and tend to the weeds in the garden. Griff followed Chase to the back shed and Sammy followed Reagan. Emma smiled to herself. Maybe things would be okay.

Chase worked for an hour in the warm sun. His head still felt cloudy, but the physical labor of tending to the garden warmed his muscles. The kinks from last night's restless sleep were working their way out. He gathered the load of weeds he had pulled and put them in the small cart. Griff happily trotted behind him as Chase left the gated garden and started down the path to the bog. When they reached the edge of the bog, Chase unloaded the cart of weeds into the mulch pile. Griff sniffed around, investigating all the new scents from the night before. Suddenly, he stiffened. A low growl sounded in his throat. Surprised, Chase looked down at his dog,

"What's the matter, boy? What's got you worked up this morning?". Chase looked out over the bog, following Griff's gaze, but couldn't see anything that looked out of place. Griff glanced up at Chase, then lowered his nose to the ground and took off through the bog, following the scent. Chase watched him go, unworried. Griff often liked to chase the rabbits that lived in the copse of trees near the bog. As Chase turned the cart and headed back toward the garden, a searing pain ripped through his head. Too much sun and no water, Chase thought. He rubbed his temples trying to ease the pain.

After drinking a glass of water and swallowing two aspirin, Chase pulled the lawnmower out of the garage and started to trim the grass.

Emma paused while working in the soap shed. She glanced out the window and saw Chase mowing the lawn. An uneasy feeling passed through her. Reagan looked up and followed Emma's gaze.

"What is Chase doing?" she asked, breaking Emma's concentration.

"He's mowing the grass, why?"

"What is that he's using?" asked Reagan.

Emma laughed, "Haven't you ever seen an old-fashioned rotary lawn mower? It doesn't have an engine. When you push it, the blades turn and cut the grass. It's quiet and gives Chase a good workout." Emma continued to watch her son, still feeling uneasy. She saw him reach to his head a couple of times, rubbing his temples. "I'll be right back. Keep stirring, please." Emma nodded to the soap mixture. Reagan turned her attention back to the soap, stirring carefully. She yawned. The lack of sleep was catching up with her.

"Chase, are you okay?". Emma tapped her son on the shoulder, getting him to pull his earbuds out.

"I'm sorry, Mom. What did you say?".

"I asked if you were okay."

"Yeah, but I have a terrible headache. I took some aspirin and drank a bunch of water, but it didn't help."

"Why don't you go lay down. The grass can wait until it's cooler this evening." Chases started to protest but realized his mom was right. He put the lawnmower away and headed to the cottage. Emma watched him go, the uneasy feeling growing within her.

Reagan helped Emma pour the soap into the molds, the fragrance of rosemary, sage, and lavender filled the room. Emma pressed lavender buds into the top of the soaps and set the molds on the racks to cure. Together they cleaned up the soap shed, putting everything away. Reagan stifled another yawn.

"I think you need to go take a nap, just like Chase. In fact, I think we all should sleep the afternoon away. What do you think?"

"I think it sounds like the perfect idea. Come on, Sammy, do you want to take a nap, too?". The puppy rolled onto his back, waving his paws in the air. Reagan laughed and crouched down to rub her puppy's soft belly.

"He loves you and trusts you. Do you know that?"

"How do you know?"

"Because he lets you keep him on his back. That is a very dangerous position for a dog. All of his vital organs are exposed. He is telling you that he knows you are the boss, and he accepts that. You are well on your way to being a wonderful dog mom."

Reagan gathered her puppy in her arms, inhaling his sweet smell. He was the one thing right about this summer. Well, her puppy and Chase. Chase was pretty right, too. Emma caught the vibe and smiled a sad smile at the girl. The summer's end was going to bring heartbreak to her son and to Reagan.

Reagan put Sammy in his crate and gave him his chew toy, then she stretched out on her bed. She was asleep in seconds.

Emma checked in on her son. Chase was sleeping with a scowl on his face. His forehead was deeply lined with worry. She reached out, gently smoothing her fingers over his forehead, chanting softly. He sighed in his sleep, his face relaxing. He rolled over, clutching his pillow in his arms and started softly snoring.

Emma walked back on the porch and gave a low whistle for Griff. She waited for a minute for him to come running, but he didn't. It wasn't the first time he'd been gone for a couple of hours, roaming the bog and scaring up the wildlife. She put fresh water in the bowl on the porch, then closed and locked the cottage door. She, too was tired. A nap was in order.

CHAPTER 27

*C*hase woke with a start. The room felt cool, a light breeze blew across his cheeks. He brushed his hand across his face. He could have sworn there had been a small paw there, softly caressing the side of his chin. He shook off the dream and stretched. His headache was a little better. He slid into his shoes and quietly crept out of his room. The cottage was silent. Looking in Reagan's room, he saw she was sleeping soundly. A quick glance in his mom's room revealed the same situation there. He got a glass of water and looked out the window. The half-mowed lawn bothered him. He was glad the mower didn't have an engine because it wouldn't wake the others. Chase took two more aspirin and went back outside.

He finished the backyard and moved to the front. He was lost in thought and, at first, didn't notice the girl who stood by their mailbox down at the road. Sensing something, he looked up and was taken by surprise. She was tall and thin and had remarkable long dark hair that curled softly along the length. As he got closer, he could see her tear-stained cheeks and her stunning beauty. She was breathtaking despite her odd clothing. She wore a strange outfit of baggy men's trousers and a torn off-white button up shirt. The sleeves were rolled up to her elbows. She seemed to be concentrating on the address on his mailbox. She looked up and glanced up and down the road. She looked terribly lost and frightened.

Chase left the lawnmower and walked down the lane toward the mailbox. The girl's head was bowed. He didn't see her sly smile as he grew closer.

"Hey, are you okay?"

She looked up, tears rolling down her face. She shook her head, then bowed down, looking at the ground.

"Are you hurt? Were you in an accident of something?" Chase looked for a car, but he didn't see anything. By now he was standing in front of her. She didn't move, just kept her head down, crying quietly.

"Hey," Chase reached a tentative hand toward her. "I'm not going to hurt you." Gently, he placed his hand under her chin and lifted her face.

Noooo. Emma sat stark upright. Something was wrong. Something was very wrong. Trying to push down the panic, she closed her eyes and concentrated. What was it? Come on, but her mind was fuzzy. She took a deep breath and tried harder. The air was fresh, so fresh.

Her eyes flew open, and she looked to the window. It was opened slightly. That shouldn't be. It had been closed and sealed with the spell, but now it was open. She got up and hurried to Reagan's room. The girl still slept, her window closed tightly. Chase. Emma rushed to Chase's room. It was empty. The window stood open. Then Emma knew. Ariana.

Chase's fingers gently pressed into the girl's chin, lifting slowly, coaxing her.

"I promise I won't hurt you. How can I help you? It's going to be okay." The girl's stopped resisting his fingers. Her face lifted to his. She opened her dry eyes and looked deeply into his. In the bog, a dog howled mournfully.

Emma fumbled in her desk, her fingers seeking the small button behind the top center drawer which lay carelessly on the floor. Pressing on the small wooden nub, Emma waited until a panel in the knee hole opened sideways. Emma carefully reached in the small space and snatched a tall, thin glass bottle. The label, brittle and brown with age, flaked onto the floor. Ancient scribbles and sketches adorned the label, the glass stopper seated firmly in the top. Emma held the bottle up to the light. A sickly yellow syrup stuck to the neck of the bottle, while a lighter amber liquid swirled in the bottom. Without stopping for shoes, Emma ran out of the cottage clutching the antique bottle to her chest.

Chase felt his soul fall forward, drowning in the inky darkness of the girl's eyes. He felt like he was losing himself to her. Surprised, he tried to pull himself away, but he couldn't. His gaze was locked with hers. A bead of sweat formed on his right temple, and the searing headache he had earlier deepened, penetrating the center of his brain, setting off firework explosions behind his eyes. He desperately wanted to squeeze them shut, but he was powerless. He couldn't break the gaze that held him, bonded him to the girl. She reached up with her right hand, caressing the back of his neck, carefully and firmly drawing him closer to her. He gasped at the coldness of her touch.

Emma looked around wildly, trying to find her son. She had heard Griff's mournful howl, and she prayed she wasn't too late. Where was he? She closed her eyes again, willing her second sight to service her in her time of need. Her eyes snapped open, and she rounded the porch. She looked down the driveway. There he was. A wretched, rotting corpse of a girl was pulling her son into her aura.

Chase felt himself drawn closer to her. His heart was pounding, squeezing pain in his chest. Trickles of sweat rolled down his spine as he struggled to breathe. He was mesmerized by her beauty, and he felt a deep desire to kiss her, to consume her. Somewhere, deep in his soul, a warning sounded to resist her, but it was hopeless. He was meant to be with this beautiful creature. Her lips, so soft, so sensual, were begging to be crushed by his. He felt himself succumbing to the pressure on his neck that was pulling him closer and closer to her.

"Chase, no!" Emma screamed. Ariana turned and hissed at Emma. Emma began to run. Then Ariana grinned, hideously and triumphantly drawing Chase into her embrace. He fell toward her, bringing his arms around her tiny waist. He drew her to him and she raised her lips to his, eager for the kiss she knew he would deliver.

"No!" Emma screamed again, as she un-stoppered the ancient bottle. A vile stench filled the air. Chase gasped as the odor reached his nostrils, causing him to stumble backward. Ariana turned toward Emma, her face a hideous mask of anger. Emma raised her arm and flung the contents of the bottle toward Ariana, covering her with the disgusting contents. Some of it splashed on Chase's arm and he yelped as the liquid seared his flesh. Ariana staggered, but recovered quickly. Her skin smoked where the liquid covered her, her flesh blistering and instantly oozing, turning into strands of rotting meat as it dripped to the ground.

Emma chanted ancient tongues as fast as she could. She averted her eyes from Ariana's and refused to look at her son as she continued to whisper, desperately trying to remember everything she had ever been taught, the litany that had been handed down through the years from all her ancestors in case this day ever came.

With her eyes closed, Emma didn't see Ariana straighten up, nor did she see Chase move once again into her embrace. Ariana locked both rotting, blistering arms around him and brought her decaying lips against his. Chase felt his emotions melting, then curiously start to die, as if he no longer cared about anything at all. His soul tried to fight, willing him not to go, but he was being dragged into the darkness that was Ariana. Her kiss deepened, drawing him in...

"No, you don't, you bitch. Let him go!" Reagan grabbed Ariana by the arm. Reagan didn't flinch as handfuls of rotting flesh came off of the bones. Ariana turned to Reagan, her black eyes flashing dangerously.

"He's mine. I already have him," Ariana cackled.

"No, you don't," screamed Reagan, as she buried the starfish pendant in Ariana's rotten heart.

CHAPTER 28

I am going to hell," Emma said, sadly. She measured the herbs carefully into the boiling liquid.

"No, you aren't. You are taking care of the people you love with the gifts you have."

"This didn't work well last time," Emma said, desperately.

"We were kids. Your gifts weren't developed, and you had a lot to learn. You're older and your skills as a healer are strong."

"I hope so. I feel wrong doing this, but I think this is the only way they will both heal."

"Will they remember anything?" asked Willow.

"Only what we want them to," said Emma. She carried two cups of tea over to the two teenagers who sat shell-shocked on the couch. "Here. Reagan. Chase. Drink this, then get some sleep. I promise you will feel better in the morning." As they drank, Willow and Emma told them stories of their summer, adding some details and leaving out others. Soon, Chase and Reagan's eyes were heavy. They slept.

EPILOGUE

*I*s Sammy settled okay back there?" asked Reagan's mom as they turned off the country road and onto the freeway ramp.

"Yeah. Luckily, he's still small and fits okay in that travel crate. He is doing so well on his potty training he hardly needs it, but he'll be safer in his little portable den."

"Did you have a good summer?"

"Yep, it was great. After all, I found the best friend ever. Sammy is wonderful. Thanks for letting me get him."

"I think he is pretty good, too. I'm sorry it was such a lonely summer. You were pretty isolated out there at Willow's. I'm sorry there weren't many people your age."

"It's okay. I met a couple of kids. They were nice and everything, but I was the odd man out, just here for the summer. I did get a lot of reading in, and just relaxed, you know? I'm glad you could come home early. It was a nice surprise."

"Do you think you would like to come back here again, just to visit? I want to stay in contact with Willow. After all, she is your dad's sister. It seems like we should keep up with the family. Don't you think?"

"Yeah, maybe that is a good idea. I feel like I have some unfinished business here, but I don't know what it is."

"Maybe it's that cute boy. What was his name? Chase or something like that?"

"Yeah, Chase. He seems nice. His mom seems nice, too. I really appreciate that they came over with that salve for Sammy's cut. I'll be honest. That boy was easy on the eyes. I only met him once or twice, but I think he's a good person. Maybe, if we come back, I'll get to know him better."

"So, I was thinking of doing some sightseeing on the long drive home, like taking a mini vacation together. Are you up for it?"

"Sure, as long as we can take Sammy wherever we go. What were you thinking?"

"I have always wanted to go to Salem, Massachusetts. Does that sound good?"

"Um, Mom, that's not, 'on the way home,' but yeah. It sounds great."

Reagan and her mom meandered down the coast, enjoying the time catching up with each other. Reagan's mom had great stories of her time oversees with the troops, and Reagan told her mom about Cora Rose's amazing cooking. They talked about trying some of the recipes Cora Rose had given Reagan when she left.

When they reached Salem, they played tourist, seeing all the typical sights. Both of them fell silent as they gazed at the Salem Witch Trials Memorial on the edge of The Old Burying Point. Reagan felt uneasy as she stared at the names. Something was tugging at the back of her memory. Shrugging it off she turned away, Sammy following at her heels. They walked to the Waterfront and wandered in and out of the shops, laughing at some of the silly witch souvenirs.

At one of the shops, Reagan and her mom bought some artisan soap, and they discovered some of Willow's pottery on the shelves. They marveled at the exquisite designs.

"It's funny. Willow is kind of gruff and rough, but her pottery is beautiful and delicate. It's strange how you don't always see the other side of people if they don't let you," mused Reagan.

They passed an antique shop when Reagan suddenly stopped.

"What's wrong?"

"Nothing, I… I just really want to go in there."

"Okay, but I didn't know you were into antiques."

"I'm not," said Reagan, "but maybe living at Willow's and being surrounded by them has me curious. Let's go in."

They wandered around looking at the beautiful old things, exclaiming at the prices. Reagan wandered to a case of old jewelry. Gazing inside, her eyes fell upon a pedant.

"What did you find?" her mom asked.

"Look at that starfish pendant. I love it."

"Would you like to see something?" An old woman with long blonde hair wearing a weird flowered caftan pulled a key from her pocket.

"Yes, that starfish pendant right there."

The lady opened the case. Sammy whimpered, softly.

"Oh, I think Sammy has to go outside."

"I'll take him," said her mom. "Take your time and look all you want."

Her mom scooped up Sammy and headed for the door. The lady handed Reagan the pendant.

"This is very old. I had it checked by an expert. He said this was handmade, probably by a sailor or a ship's captain. See the intricate knots on the string? Those are knots that sailors used to use on the big old sailing ships. It's really a unique piece, and the string is in remarkably good shape for its age."

"I'll take it," said Reagan opening her wallet and extracting several bills.

"Hold on, I'll wrap it for you."

"No thanks, I'll just wear it." Reagan turned from the counter and placed the necklace around her neck.

"Here, let me help you." Delicate fingers tied the ancient strings. The beautiful blonde lady smiled as the starfish settled on Reagan's chest. Reagan lifted her fingers to touch the starfish, feeling strangely comforted as the black metal warmed her flesh.

DID YOU ENJOY THE STARFISH TALISMAN?

Thank you for taking time to read my book, The Starfish Talisman. It was a hoot to write. One night I had to quit writing and hide under the covers, because I had spooked myself. All the years of listening to my mom tell about the wolves under the dining room table must have given me the willies!

If you enjoyed the book, please take the time to review it. Reviews are what help authors stay alive to write another story. Please leave your review on Amazon and Goodreads.

Thank you and journey on,

Lark

ACKNOWLEDGMENTS

I want to thank all of the people who made this book possible, especially my mom for telling me the stories of the house on Crittenden Avenue and the wolves she used to see under the dining room table.

I also want to thank my teen readers Alexis, Charlie, and Char, and my adult readers Joe and Mary. Their encouragement and suggestions are always appreciated.

Jennifer Sivec also deserves mention. She has helped me so much on my journey to create my stories. She always responds to my messages for help, no matter what time or how bizarre.

I used a new editor for this book, J.C. Wing of Wing Family Editing. Thanks J.C. for helping me get to the next level. I am forever grateful for your encouragement and corrections.

Finally, I want to thank my husband, Joe, and my son, Charlie for tolerating all the evenings when I monopolized the couch and wrote for hours, or those times in the front of the truck on a road trip when you graciously turned off the radio and suffered in silence as I wrote. I love you guys. You are my life.

ALSO BY LARK GRIFFING

The Last Time I Checked I Was Still Here

The Last Time I Checked, I Was Still Here is a coming of age adventure novel. Turn the page for a sneak peek.

The Last Time I Checked, I Was Still Here

LARK GRIFFING

THE LAST TIME I CHECKED, I WAS STILL HERE

1

AMY

The socks were the last straw, the breaking point. Despite all the heartache and abuse, the stupid socks are what did it. The socks made her leave.

Amy wound her way through the trees, taking the long way to the school. The sidewalks were the way to travel, but Amy wasn't having any of that. The sidewalks led past Ronnie's house, and you could bet Ronnie and the Ronnettes would be there, waiting for her, ready to pounce. It had been that way since the beginning of the year when Amy started her senior year at Maplewood High. Just another school in another place after a long line of schools. This one was the worst, however.

Usually Amy could fade into the woodwork. She was an average student, with, what she considered, average looks. Her transient nature made it difficult for her to make real, lasting friendships, except for Betsy. Betsy was three schools ago, and she was special. She was one of those people who could look into your soul and get you. Betsy got Amy. They became friends and that was that. Then, of course, Amy moved. Her dad got another transfer to supervise the building of another superstore, and off they went. Mom would never have let that happen, but Mom was gone and dad was lost, running from one job to another, filling his life, drowning the empty spaces that had been his beloved wife.

So, this morning, the morning of the socks, left Amy bush-whacking her way through the park, around the spreading maples that shaded the woods. Once she broke free of the trees, she had to traipse through the meadow until she reached the school. If all worked as planned, she would avoid a meeting of Ronnie and her bevy of friends. Amy sighed. It was pathetic that this group of small town girls wanted so badly to be the up and coming mean girls. They were good at it, and Amy was tired of it.

She slipped into the cool hallways and slid around the stair-well to her locker. That was the best thing about this school. Her locker was hidden in a cramped alcove behind a stairwell. It kept her out of the main flow of traffic. She preferred it that way, not being interested in funneling to class with the in crowd. Amy just wanted to be left alone. She stowed her hoodie on the hook in the locker and grabbed books and for her first three classes.

She turned around and bumped smack dab into Ronnie and the Ronnettes.

"Hey, skank." Ronnie looked Amy up and down, appraising her outfit, her hair, her whatever. Amy ignored her and tried to move around her to head to class. "I'm talking to you skank-girl," said Ronnie.

"What is it you so desperately need, Ronnie?" Amy asked, her eyes steady on Ronnie's.

"Nothing, just wanted to wish you a good morning."

"Oh my God! Check out at her socks," squealed Fawn. Fawn was the outlier in the Ronnettes. She didn't look like she fit in with the spray of pimples across her forehead and her slightly jutting, not yet brace adjusted upper front teeth. Her daddy, however, owned the local movie theater, and Fawn could get all her friends in free. Instant popularity for the not so pretty girl. "What's all over her stupid socks?"

Amy looked down with the rest of them. Her socks were covered in burrs, each clinging to the fabric like tiny porcupines. There were burrs upon burrs stuck to her, bunching the bottoms of her jeans in an unnatural manner. Amy could feel her face burning with heat. The meadow. In order to escape Ronnie and the Ronnettes, Amy had cut through that meadow. She was concentrating so hard on not being seen, she didn't even notice the hitchhikers that made their home on her socks. The girls surrounding her began to laugh and jeer. Amy, with her face burning even hotter, shoved her way through the group and headed to class. She wouldn't let them have the satisfaction of knowing they really got to her this time. She would not dissolve into tears.

She dropped her books on her desk in Mrs. Parcher's class, mumbled a quick, "I need to go to the bathroom," and then made her escape around the corner into the ladies' room. There, she shut herself in a stall and began the painful process of removing all the burrs.

It didn't go well. Each time she tried to pull a burr off, it split in half and left individual barbs embedded in her socks. Not only were they unsightly, but they worked themselves deeper into the fabric and began to rub uncomfortably at her ankle. She was doomed. She kept picking at them, oblivious to the time slipping away. She didn't want to head back to class with the remaining burrs still clinging to her socks or digging into her flesh.

"Hey, um, Amy, are you okay?" asked a voice Amy didn't recognize. "Mrs. Parcher thinks you've been in here for a long time and is worried that something is wrong. So, God this is embarrassing, are you like, okay?"

"I'm fine, thank you. Please tell her I'll be out in a minute. I'm sorry you had to come check on me, even though I can't see who you are."

"It's Ginny, and no worries. Actually, it's better than listening to old Parcher droning on about reconstruction of the South."

"Good point," Amy said. She opened the door of the stall and stepped out. Her face was red from bending over so long and there was a handful of burrs and sock fuzz mashed up in her palm.

"What the hell is that?" said Ginny. Amy realized, too late, that she should have flushed the whole mess down the toilet.

"Okay, so I took a shortcut through the meadow trying to avoid Ronnie and the Ronnettes and got burrs stuck in my socks." Amy realized her gaffe as soon as it left her mouth.

"Ronnie and the Ronnettes? That's hilarious." Oh great, thought Amy, by lunch the whole school will know. Ginny was a nice girl, but her tragic flaw was that she could not keep her mouth shut. This day was getting worse by the minute. Amy gave one last tug at the bottom of her jeans and headed out of the bathroom. She could still hear Ginny muttering about the new girl band. Amy's heart sank when she saw the flash of Ginny's cell phone and knew it was all over. Ginny couldn't wait to share all the gory details.

Amy stayed slumped in her chair for the rest of Parcher's monologue on the South after the war and escaped the minute the bell rang. She had been thinking for the last thirty minutes what she could do to minimize the damage, but there was just no hope. Her life was going to super suck from this moment on.

The bell rang, dismissing the class. Amy gathered her things and began to walk to her next class, but then passed it and went out the side door of the school instead. She hit the meadow with a purposeful gait. This time, she recognized the tearing of the burrs at her socks, but that didn't stop her. She was done. She was over this town, this place, this life, and things were going to change.

To continue reading, click the link:
    The Last Time I Checked, I Was Still Here

ABOUT THE AUTHOR

Lark Griffing spins stories. She has two young adult novels published and is currently working on a women's fiction series. This is Lark's second book.

www.ingramcontent.com/pod-product-compliance
Lightning Source LLC
Chambersburg PA
CBHW021010120726
47905CB00009B/2942